Please, San Antonio! & Melisande in Paris

Two Novellas, Special International Edition

Please, San Antonio! & *Melisande in Paris*

Two Novellas, Special International Edition

By

Eve La Salle Caram

and

Cecilia Manguerra Brainard

Illustrations by Nina Lim-Yuson

PALH
P.O. Box 5099
Santa Monica, CA 90409
USA
2018

Please, San Antonio! & *Melisande in Paris:*
Two Novellas, Special International Edition

Copyright © 2018 by Cecilia Manguerra Brainard
    & Eve La Salle Caram

All rights reserved. No part of this book may be used or reproduced in any manner or form without permission by the authors and publisher, except in the form of brief quotations embodied in critical articles or reviews.

Published by PALH (Philippine American Literary House)
P.O. Box 5099
Santa Monica, CA 90409
USA
http://www.palhbooks.com
Email: palh@aol.com

First Edition

Library of Congress Control Number: 2017919169
ISBN 978-0-9719458-8-3

Acknowledgments:

Illustrations by Nina Lim-Yuson, Copyright © 2018 by
    Nina Lim-Yuson
Book Design by C. Sophia Ibardaloza

"The goal of life is rapture...One looks at the world
and sees the Radiance..."
—Joseph Campbell

Please, San Antonio!

Eve La Salle Caram

"To Bethel and Neil
in memory of our Italian adventure."

San Antonio, please. Please find my orange pencil and the pink one. I was making such a picture with them.

The Sun Queen. Or part of her. I have an altar to her in our back yard and when I kneel before it and spread my fingers across my eyes I can see some of her.

I can see part of her wings.

When Beatrice was seven or eight she had petitioned the saint and before the morning was out found her missing pencils, the color of nasturtiums and roses, underneath the leaf of a speckled canna where the wind from Corpus Christi Bay had blown them. She wasn't

Catholic, but her Mexican friend, Consuela, who was, told her that San Antonio would always find whatever she lost—and he had. He had found those pencils that in her hands had made a replica of the Sun Queen's wings—one so striking that her teacher had praised it and posted it on a bulletin board in front of the room for everyone in her third grade class to see.

Later, on the day when she was home sick with the flu, when she asked him to find an arm that had come off her doll, the arm had all at once appeared from under the corner of the blanket on her bed. Then she remembered how she had clutched it to her when she coughed and she reasoned—for she was old enough to reason—that, during a bad dream in sleep, she must have pulled it out of its socket.

Over the years, San Antonio—who by the time she was a teenager was as real as the Sun Queen had been to her when she was seven and eight—found every object she had ever lost—or so it seemed. Her drawing pencils. The arm of her doll. The book of Roman myths she loved. The multi colored pieces of construction paper she had threaded together with tinsel to make decorations for a school Christmas play. But when she was older she asked San Antonio if he could find lost persons, those who had moved far away from her and whose whereabouts she had lost track of and even more impossible, those who had died.

Facebook didn't bring them back and Google had nothing on them.

No, she told herself, childhood and magical thinking were gone—there was no way to bring them back and, never mind, that as an adult she had several Catholic friends who still implored San Antonio (who they thought of as Saint Anthony) to find what was lost. Objects, of course, she told herself. Not talents (she no longer drew). Not people.

"Tony, Tony," she heard them say, "please come round. Something is lost and must be found."

Now that more than half her life was gone and she was entering her senior years, she couldn't ask Saint Anthony to simply look for a lost drawing pencil—she would have to ask him to restore her ability—and even her will—to draw.

And the one who had first taught her, the practitioner—the artist who had encouraged her when she was twenty—had died. Had been caught outside in a rain storm after leaving the studio on their college campus where she taught, had the next day woken up with a sore throat and a fever, was hospitalized in New York and died.

After graduation she had lived in New York. Then Florida, Louisiana and finally, Los Angeles where various schools and jobs had brought her. And by mid-life she had lost more than that first great teacher. Friends, some of them very dear (one of breast cancer when she was only thirty-three and the new mother of a six-month-old child, a little girl). Men she might have lived with or married (one of them killed in a war). The man she did marry—through separation?—she couldn't quite remember—what had happened to him?—where did he go? They had no children and she had grown up the only child of a single mother. Now her mother as well as a beloved grandfather and uncles and aunts were gone—she had lost her mother early—and with all of them her will to draw, to work in colored pencil or in watercolor. She taught others sometimes—a stint as an art teacher here, another, there. Nothing full time or steady had ever come along, and worst of all—something she would not say aloud to any student, to anyone, she no longer took out the pencils or watercolors (or even chalk) herself.

On Christmas Eve a neighbor in the apartment building where she lived and who knew how she felt, drove down Sunset to the great new "People's Cathedral" in Los Angeles, Our Lady of the Angels, where she bought a little Saint Anthony statue and gave it to her. "He's beautiful," Beatrice said and later she placed him with the objects, also beautiful, she had collected (and also considered "beautiful") from the sea. The shells from her Texas childhood—Padre Island, Galveston—along with those from Florida, from Louisiana's Grand Isle and from the coves of Laguna she so loved to visit in California. From Hawaii, even.

And yes—finally—from Italy. Amalfi. And a small, brown beach near Sorrento where she had been told she would not find shells.

So now she not only said, "Please San Antonio," she also said, "Please San Antonino."

What a surprise in Sorrento where she had been the summer before, Saint Anthony, her San Antonio, had become San Antonino!

When she saw the statue in the square with the plaque underneath she was stunned. San Antonino. No wonder when she set out for Italy, no wonder she had wanted to go to Sorrento most of all. Her San Antonio—now San Antonino—was there. And yes, in her guidebook she discovered he was for some reason—what?—the patron saint of the town.

Before him she became a child again.

"Please San Antonio—please—can you find those I loved? Can you in some way bring them back? And can you bring back my will to somehow follow my teacher's example to make art? To labor at my craft? To try for something greater?"

("Radiance" was what she wanted to say but couldn't. "Radiance."... And something else, something of it or through it—what?)

Perhaps the one she had known as San Antonio had purposefully brought her to Italy, to the country where he had lived most of his life. She now clearly saw he was San Antonino—of Padua, yes. But, mysteriously, also of Sorrento.

And, of course, also of her heart.

Chapter 2

Why Sorrento?—the question she asked herself when she arrived. And she didn't know. Among the many Saint Anthony protected were seafarers. She had read that.

Winds of great force had, after all, blown his ship headed for his home in Portugal—after his mission in Africa, where he had contracted a sickness, was cut short—east across the Mediterranean to Sicily where monks from the town of Messina rescued him and nursed him back to health and later sent him on his way to a conference in Italy, after which Italy became his home. His own earlier plan, when he was just a teenager, to be a martyred monk in Morocco had been altered by his sickness, then by nature. Italy healed him and when he was well, and given an assignment in Padua by Saint Frances, he gave sermons so eloquent and in a voice so beautiful even the fish jumped when they heard him and those who had deafened themselves to his music, when they saw the fish, unplugged their hearing and listened.

But, Sorrento? She had not read of him in Sorrento and it never occurred to her that there might be more than one Saint Anthony, (her San Antonio). When she entered the church she read that San Antonino protected those tossed by the ocean's winds.

After all, she thought, he himself had been. That tossing had, in fact, brought him to this country. He was, she read, also the champion of many others, especially the poor and the sick—and travelers.

She had come to Italy to see both the art and the renowned beauty of the country. This peninsula, this coast especially. She was, after all, OF coasts. The one in Texas where she had grown up and the ones on the Gulf side when she had lived in Florida and Louisiana, and, of course, the one on which she lived now in California. She was a coastal person she told herself so it was natural when she came to Italy for her to want to be on the most renowned section of its coast. Still, when she ventured into the central square—the Piazza—of Sorrento—a city which she had not researched, which she knew only from its famed popular song and the travel posters about it, she was shocked to find the statue of Saint Anthony, her (she believed) San Antonio—here, San Antonino—at its heart.

And, she had asked, why are you here? You who are known to be of Padua so far to the north and east? No one in her party—art students and others (an oddly mixed group that had come together to take advantage of this particularly economical travel package)—knew or seemed much to care. They were only interested in their immediate surroundings and in going to Capri.

"Beverly Hills on a hill," she had been told, "and surrounded by water. Don't get your hopes up for it." Still, she had eyes. When she looked across the expanse of variegated blue she could see its beauty. Never mind the expensive boutiques. Chanel. Armani. She could see the island from the terrace of her hotel. She looked forward to the boat ride to it.

"Boat rides are so boring," the large woman sitting across from her said. "I haven't taken a boat ride in twenty years. I had forgotten how boring they are."

Beatrice couldn't answer, couldn't look at her. Looked out, instead, over the water. Cobalt blue, streaked with green, with turquoise. Made her want to reach for the drawing pencils she had not brought with her—the first time she had had such an intense urge to use them in years.

"Oh, how boring!" the woman said again.

Who was she? Surely not one of the art students in their group. She had not yet met them all. She knew it was a larger group than she should have joined (the more people along when traveling, the more dissension there was likely to be), but it was inexpensive because of the number and she needed to be careful with money. She would have to keep reminding herself of that. Who could this person possibly be?

"Boring," the woman continued to mutter under her breath.

Some rebuttal, Beatrice thought, must be made and the most effective would be in paint or pastels or watercolor. There was film, of course, and like everyone else she had brought a camera and could also take pictures on her phone. But now she wished for more, wished for her drawing pencils. The guide was pointing out the president's summer house and the many arches—one with a Madonna inside, the greenish-white stone gleaming. Greenery poking through rock speckled with minerals glittering in the sun.

Chapter 3

When they had all first arrived and she had seen the statue of San Antonio in Sorrento's Piazza she thought surely she had been directed. That it was not only to paint or draw that she had come to this location.

But no! Rather than directed, she had been deluded. This San Antonio—San Antonino—was not the same one who had long ago found her drawing pencils. There were other San Antoninos. When she searched with her laptop she found them. A trio. (And, who knew, if she went on searching maybe three times three?) So far she had found not only Saint Anthony of Padua but Saint Anthony of Egypt who the others, perhaps had been named after, a monk who meditated and prayed in caves, father of all monastic orders, and the one in the Sorrento Piazza from Compania, born hundreds of years earlier than St. Anthony of Padua.

San Antonio who was the finder of both lost objects and, or so the literature told her, of lost souls, was, yes, a traveling preacher and the saint of travelers as well as of seafarers. And the one who was in the Sorrento piazza was ALSO the saint of sailors and navigators, so no wonder she had taken him for HER San Antonio. Never mind the difference in years or geography, an overlap in those the saints protected was there! And both of them claimed Italia although only one of them was born there.

The one from Padua was always shown carrying the Christ Child in his arms. Or flowers. Or a book. Or all three. He had, she discovered become the finder of lost things because someone had stolen his most beloved book. A beautiful book of psalms in which he kept notes for his sermons. Then, after he had prayed it would be returned to him, the book reappeared, returned by one who had fled the order. (Oh, she thought, how once I would have loved to illustrate the book of psalms he held. I would have done it with my pencils in flaming pinks and ocher and gold.) This San Antonio was always formally referred to as "St. Anthony of Padua," for although he traveled all over Italy and some of France, that town became his home and he was buried there.

The statue in Sorrento of the Saint Anthony born hundreds of years earlier and who was entombed in the local basilica, held no book or flower or babe, but stood erect, a halo around his head—a mighty force, she thought for good, perhaps, even for direction, but not one, she supposed to ask for the return of lost objects or persons or inspiration.

And, she told herself, in reality—which you need to come back to—there is nothing—no person—not even a sainted person (or animal or plant or food or flower) who can do that for you.

This was the thought that came to her the afternoon she found herself stuck on of all beautiful places in the world, the one that was among the most beautiful, Capri with the "boat rides are so boring" person, whose name she discovered was Maggie.

Waiting for the rest of the group to return from an adventure on Anacapri where she wished she, too, had gone—she had lingered too long over a view and discovered through Maggie that the others in their party had simply taken off—she heard Maggie, who seemed to see nothing that was directly in front of her, rattling on and on about Tapas bars she had visited in Spain on her only other European adventure, when she was there several years before. Then, abruptly heard Maggie ask, "Is this all you expected?" And heard herself, who thought the views from Capri and the Sorrento peninsula the most heavenly she had ever seen, heard herself, Beatrice—she who was a lover, a worshiper even, of coasts and, yes, of views (she who had been named for the woman who led Dante to the Pinnacle Viewing Place)—heard herself say, "No. I've had a great disappointment. I was hoping for more."

She couldn't add, "I was hoping Sorrento's saint would be a finder." One who could bring back all that had connected her to a radiance that was now gone.

Why had she been so angry?

After being with Maggie only a short time she realized that Maggie had many distressing physical problems that were absolutely real. Problems that prevented her from going to Anacapri with the others, problems that forced the group to cut short their time spent on the island, and cut out a dinner they had planned on

Anacapri, in a restaurant where they were told the view of the moonrise each evening was the most beautiful on earth and that she had certainly wanted to see. Problems that included an enlarged heart, an underactive thyroid, digestive difficulties. A stomach tumor had recently been removed, but now another grew in its place. Bea also realized that Maggie hated not only her ailments, but also herself. She told Bea as they sat on that bench waiting for the others in their group to arrive that when she had gone into one of the elegant shops in the square known to tourists as "Beverly Hills on a Hill" (a short walk from the top of the funicular) the sales person had said, "Oh, nothing for YOU, Madam." Maggie laughed the remark off when she told it, but clearly it was one that stung. Worse. Probably one that wounded.

Where was Bea's compassion? She said nothing in response.

But, she told herself, she had at least begun to think of this big woman (burdened by at least a hundred pounds she didn't need to carry) by the name everyone called her. "Maggie" was probably originally Margaret. She didn't think Margaret would have told the story about the salesperson's remark the way Maggie had, which Bea only took as a bid for attention. She couldn't smile or laugh —or say what she actually wanted to feel. I am so sorry. So sorry that you feel compelled to tell this story—that you may even have set out to find this story to tell. Knowing that Maggie could hardly wait to leave Capri, to once again be lying in her bed back at the hotel—or even better the one in her house in Ohio—Bea had only said, "I would like to stay here. I would like to go to the other side of this island and eat in that dining room we all heard about. I would like to see the moon rise over Anacapri—the most beautiful moonrise—or so I've heard—in the world."

Maggie's turn to be silent.

OK because members of the group who had been on various adventures began to return and gather round them and before they knew it, they were back on a boat which under the stars cut its way across the Tyrrhenian sea.

That night in her dream not one St. Anthony but two appeared before her, the one with the halo, a local, and the other (a good distance and to one side behind him) the one with the child in his arms and in one hand, a book and a lily. In spite of his halo, or maybe because of it, the one nearest to her said, "Drive a straight course." And the one far behind him—the one with the flower, the book, the child, asked, "What have you lost?"

And in the dream she had answered, "I have lost my compassion."

And she had awakened wondering, have I? Over the years of pain and losses has my heart hardened? Is that why I can't make the beautiful colored pictures I could make when I was young (she was now past sixty)—could make even when I was a child? Is that why I can't break through with empathy to, and maybe even help, for the woman who lets herself be called Maggie, who has forgotten that she was once Margaret?

After the second St. Anthony had spoken to her she thought she had seen him open his book and she remembered from her own reading that he was a lover of words, that because of his understanding of them, and because he felt them resonate, he moved many with his speaking—even that a school of fish in the Adriatic jumped when he spoke. Maybe through him, through his words about what he found in his book she could get back what was now gone from her.

But, she then told herself, if I have lost my compassion I don't believe I can get it back through reading. Or even through direct petition. She wasn't, after all, now looking for lost drawing pencils, or even for lost connections, but for an open place in her heart.

Chapter 4

The drawing she began was of the sunrise she witnessed the night after she had the dream. A rim of black, then light blue, a darker blue, an azure. Then pink, a darker pink, a sizzling bright one—and then, surprisingly, a beige. And, finally, the large egg yolk of the sun rising. A sunrise—not a moonrise, like the one she had wanted to see, and to maybe capture something of —over Anacapri. But a sunrise she had seen, after a night when she couldn't sleep, right here in her room. Crude, yes. The pencil drawing she told herself of a child.

Yet the picture pulled her into it and took her through the blackness into the labyrinth of blues and then pinks that bordered on apricots and oranges, then through the circle of darker color (a beige brown) and deposited her, finally, on the scarlet mountain of the sun—a long journey that left her so drained that at last she dropped her colored pencils, along with the pad on which she had made her picture, and fell upon the sofa near the chair where she had been drawing into a deep sleep. And then after a long time—near morning, and another sunrise, another dream.

In the dream all those who had died stood before her: her mother, a lover, her husband, her friend with the baby girl, then her beloved teacher who, like her friend, had also died young and two of the San Antoninos—the one of Padua—still holding his lilies and his lost book—and the one with a halo so in tune with nature and all in the natural world, directing navigators of ships from Sorrento.

"We are," they said in unison, "both here to guide you." And then they told her to travel—to the north and east—Rome, first of course, then Florence—and perhaps, when she had the means and the time, beyond. And, then once again to the south, Sorrento, with Capri in sight. There she might also realize that everybody and everything she had loved and lost was once again hers, had come back to her—that she had been literally

GIFTED ABUNDANTLY in THE MOST BEAUTIFUL PLACE IN THE WORLD.

    She saw the letters that spelled that message out in all Caps before her. The title, she told herself, of my dream. When she was a child her dreams often had titles.

After she woke and rose from the couch in her room in the hotel where everyone in her group was staying, she dressed and went to the dining room for breakfast with the others. The abundance of the breakfast, the same as the one that had been put out every morning since they arrived in Sorrento, suddenly struck her—why, it was a feast!—golden eggs and golden breads and salami as well as ham and five kinds of cheeses, and all those tomatoes and cucumbers and peppers, greens and reds and yellows, capers and olives (imagine! and for breakfast!). She hugged Maggie when she saw her, a surprise to both of them, and thanked her for the question she had asked the day before (the question she had at the time resented) and told her she was going to leave the group and use what savings she had accumulated to set out on a journey she had been directed to take alone.

Chapter 5

She also told herself she was probably crazy. After all, she had chosen to go with this large group to Italy because the travel package was inexpensive. Could she really forfeit what she had paid and then take on the expense and uncertainty of striking out on her own? She was not in a time of life when she could afford to use her meager savings and yet she believed her dream was a gift to her from the two San Antoninos and meant to be instructive.

As her drawing was.

When she looked at it she knew from her experience just hours before that if she used it as a kind of map for what might lie ahead it might direct her. To get to the sun she would have to walk the labyrinth out of the bottomless blackness into the circles of color—the blues, pale to azure—the faint pinks to the hottest, brightest one—then into beige, a neutral ether—but which could appear to her to be very dark. And then, the summit. A long trip. Some of it might be perilous.

All journeys are perilous she told herself. But would the beginning steps in the frightening blackness go on for a long, long time?

Then she told herself to cut it out—that she was taking her own metaphor, the one she had made up, too far.

First she was lost on a tree-lined street in Rome—in what one of the guide books called "Pilgrim's Rome" because of its churches. When she chose the street of the two she saw after she got off the tour bus at Santa Maria Maggiore she had hoped it would lead her back to her hotel—but no. It just went on and on. The bus tour which had left her at that junction had been poorly selected—yes, that she alone had selected—the commentary, all in Italian, little of which she understood. So, however impressive the buildings and monuments before her, they remained visuals only. Maybe not a bad thing for one who drew, or at least wanted to. Some, like the Pantheon, she recognized from photographs she had seen of them. But she hardly knew what others were.

"Do you speak English?" she asked the young couple standing on the corner, and was delighted when they said in unison, "Yes."

From Norway—what she thought of as the top of the world—of all places, they told her the street she was looking for was near the Colosseum and they pointed in a direction that she knew was wrong. They were, after all, northerners in a southern city, strangers to it like herself. She had been to the Colosseum and remembered its location. But she smiled and thanked them, then when they were around a corner and out of sight, turned and walked the other way.

She would retrace her steps and simply walk back the eight or nine blocks from which she had come to her starting place in front of the great church of Santa Maria Maggiore. Of course she might come across others that she could ask along the way.

The first question from a slight woman in a rumpled coat came to her, however. And although she was flattered that the woman had taken her for someone who spoke Italian she answered, "Non parlo Italiano," which, in truth, was just about as much Italian as she knew and could articulate.

In the next block she stopped in a Pharmacy to ask directions of the woman pharmacist and got easy, explicit directions in perfect English. Cross the street at the corner and continue on it and you will find yourself on the square of Victor Emmanuel and the Hotel Napoleon (her hotel).

"The name of the street I take?" she asked.

The woman shook her head and smiled. "It has no name."

Incredible, she thought, that in the Eternal City there could be any street with no name, but she realized then that there were probably numbers of them—these ghost streets. Rome, she concluded seemed a city more about visuals than the labels for them or at least that was the way she was experiencing it on this day.

Her first solo.

And she had begun it, like an actress in a movie, with a gelatto. A limone. She adored all the limones. And when the woman who served her dropped a large pile of whipped cream on top she had laughed. And had struck out, gelatto in hand, on her ill chosen way.

Now she was redirected.

Rome was softer than she had imagined. She supposed she had thought of it in terms of monuments, so that all the images that she had were of stone. But, look, she told herself. Look at the trees. So many trees. The leaves touching each other, topping every street, and brushing against the soft, faded colors of buildings, pale yellows and melons and tangerines, a few soft blues. Never mind the occasional graffiti, how worn or dirt streaked the colors, there was a softness, even a languor in the air.

Yes, this is what I remember she wanted to say. But how could she? She had never been to

Rome before in her life. And even on this first time had gotten lost. And yet she felt a familiarity she couldn't explain.

The next day near the Colosseum, under the Parasol Pines, those Felini trees, she first took pictures, and then lifted a small sketch pad out of her shoulder bag and some drawing pencils and resting against a large stone began to draw. She had expected to be overwhelmed by grandeur. Instead, language barrier or no, she simply felt at home. This is like a small town I remember she told herself, there is a homey feel under the umbrella of these trees.

The shape she was making was of a tree, yes, but a tree a child might draw. Crude as her sketch of the sunrise. Once she had been a draftsman. She was drawing and, yes, now wanted to, but where was her skill? The skill she had worked hard to develop and once possessed.

Well, she told herself, no matter. She was deeply happy as she drew.

One tree. Then another and another, (with pencils more blue than green), rows and rows of them. Then, underneath the tallest, a figure—a woman, and then, beside her, another even smaller figure. Why, she began to ask herself are these shapes so familiar?

It was not until days later when she began to do bigger sketches of this pair than she had that morning under the protection of Roman pines, her companions which she had begun to think of in almost human terms, that she began to put on paper what she never had before, although she had long wanted to, images of her friend who long ago died at sea—yes, on a vast blue-green ocean— only months after she had given birth to her little girl. Beatrice had gotten to know Frannie when they both worked, briefly, for an ad agency in New York. Then Frannie after a decade of wrong relationships finally entered into one that seemed right and she was, with her husband and baby daughter, on her way to meet her husband's family who lived in faraway Australia when she died aboard ship after a big wave struck and her heart, damaged early in her life by rheumatic fever, simply failed. Beatrice was pleased with the likeness of her friend she managed to get down on paper—crude, yes, but something of the spirit of Frannie, not just a likeness of features, seemed to be in it.

After she finished it, but still in Rome, supported by the same stone and protected by the same trees, she began to draw more figures: the lanky young man she had loved, with all the confusion and passion of a "first love"—though one never consummated—in college. In many ways they were alike—they even had the same coloring. Tall and thin with wavy hair and such sad gray eyes —although they could hold laughter, too—(she and he often laughed together) he had lost both of his parents when he was ten and the sole survivor of an accident in a private plane. He had no siblings, or even aunts and uncles—only distant cousins, generations and three or four times removed, who when he saw them were less than kind. Theirs was a powerful attraction. Once when he held her close and touched his mouth to hers, he then opened it and said. "Breathe with me." They were so much alike—friends said they even looked alike—tall and thin with light eyes (though his were grey and hers, blue). He drifted away from her somehow. She supposed it was because they were both so young and, after graduation, life had taken them to different parts of the country, he to the north, her to the south.

Then she drew the face of her friend who was killed in the Korean war. She had known him in high school. They were pals rather than would be lovers, but some people thought, before he went off to fight, that one day they might marry.

She drew her husband's face then, concentrating on the soft look around his eyes, the kindness in them. The deep lines around his mouth. She couldn't now recall how she had lost him and couldn't even hold her question about it long in her mind—the pain of losing him had been that great.

Before she left Rome she had sketches of all their faces. Those beloved who had, one way or another, vanished from her. Finally she even sketched her mother's face which she barely remembered—she had lost her mother so long ago—and those of other relatives, adored early in her life (the aunt and uncle she had lived with after her mother was gone.) And, yes, in the end, even the face of the artist who had taught her and who had, stupidly (she thought, she had been so angry!), caught cold in the rain and died.

And she continued to draw trees. Many, many trees. Trees more blue than green. Faces floating over the tops of them, or sometimes, between their branches.

She drew on the train that took her to Florence, the train that moved through the Umbrian and Tuscan hills past hilltop towns, past meadows of snowy sheep—always one or two black ones among them. She drew trees and hills and more and more faces. And when she disembarked, found herself facing the Renaissance.

Chapter 6

Art's focus on humanity, not the church, not the saints—the Doors of Paradise opened to those who did—who were—what?

As many replicas as she had seen of the David she was still shocked by the one Michelangelo had actually sculpted and she stood, stunned, before it, brought back only by the sound of a familiar voice.

"This is all I came to this country to see," the voice said.

When she turned away from the white magnificence before her she looked straight at Maggie. The tour group that she had somehow mercifully missed in Rome had arrived in Firenze, and there in front of the David she had no place to hide.

"I'm staying in a little pensionne," she heard herself explaining, as if to confess, not knowing why she felt so compelled. "I left the tour because I wanted to linger in some places. I began to draw again in Rome."

"Well," Maggie said in a loud voice, "I'm ready for this tour to end. Except for this—" (she paused to give the David a nod, but not really looking at him) "there hasn't been one thing I've wanted to see or had any interest in. Pompeii was a drag—too much walking—and Naples, lousier than even New Jersey, a slum full of pick pockets—I nearly fainted in Rome from the heat and so many of the buildings looked dirty. Disgusting, all that graffiti. Nothing like I expected, nothing." She let out a big sigh and then in an even louder voice, which made Bea cringe, cried out, "I hate Italy!"

All the old revulsion Bea thought she had overcome overtook her. She wanted to turn away from this monster and run, but said, "I'm sorry, Maggie." She was scheduled to leave for Venice, then Padua after that.

But found herself in Maggie's hotel room instead—the shades drawn, Maggie propped on pillows—a book in her hand. She had dropped from her chair to the floor of the Academia just as Bea turned to leave—a crowd around her, the tour director summoned, an ambulance called, medication, Bea was told when she inquired, ordered. Nitroglycerin, to regulate her heart.

"When I'm at home," she said, "This is the way I like to spend my days. In bed. I can read all day. I like a bright bulb in my lamp. This one is too dim. But I don't like daylight in the room." She nodded toward the room's heavy curtains. "I couldn't get those closed."

Almost against her will for she couldn't understand why Maggie, or anyone, could not want sunlight in her room, Bea found herself walking toward the heavy drapes to close them.

"I can't seem to get these to meet. Not completely," she murmured as she pulled on the blue and gold checkered material.

"It's OK," Maggie said. "This light I'm trying to read by is not very strong."

Bea slumped down in the chair across from Maggie's bed—a big double—Maggie propped upon it like a queen on a throne.

"Is there anyone in Youngstown you want me to call for you?" Bea asked. "Do you think you can finish the tour? Or do you just want to go home?"

"I'll stick the damn thing out. I'll be all right now that I'm on medication. This country nearly did me in—but I'll survive it." She laughed. "I haven't been on nitroglycerine in years!" She flipped a page in her book. (Bea couldn't see what she was reading.) "There's nobody in Youngstown or in the whole state of Ohio I give a fucking damn about. My daughter thinks I'm a freaking checkbook. She just wants what she can get out of me for herself and her ugly kids."

Something stirred inside of Bea. "You don't want me to call her?"

"A fucking NO," Maggie said.

"And there's no one else?"

"No," Maggie said. Then she pointed to her purse. "Open that, she said. "Take out my ticket for the tour of the Uffizi. Go with the group in my place."

Maggie had gifted her—and there she was before the Botticelli's—*The Birth of Venus*, *The Primivera*—which she had imagined as gigantic, but which in reality are no bigger than most middle sized paintings she had seen in many other galleries she had visited. Yet, in oil paint applied by genius, they had an ethereal other worldly glow no print could ever convey.

Maggie had gifted her with the sight of them. Maggie trapped in her hotel room, trapped in her bed. Trapped in her body.

In a room. Always—forever and ever in a room somewhere.

But that was what she wanted she had said. She wanted to be in a bed in a room, curtains closed.

She did read books. What were they? What did she take from them?

Bea wasn't sure why but she wanted to feel something for this woman. Something besides anger and pity and contempt.

Chapter 7

*B*ut that was difficult. She would go back to the hotel to say goodbye and, as a thanksgiving—and to assuage her guilt, the reason she had probably been there in the first place—give Maggie a book she had bought in the gift shop with illustrations of many paintings, especially the Botticellis and Leonardo's, and commentary on them. And then she would say goodbye.

Maggie only nodded when she took the book then dropped it to one side. "I never gave a damn about seeing anything in that place," was all she said. "I never gave a freaking damn." Then she asked for a pizza. "Find someone to bring me one," she commanded. "I can't wait for fucking room service dinner. And a gelato. Chocolate. With whipped cream on top. Have them bring me that."

The tour director shrugged when Beatrice told him. "Yesterday it was also pizza and gelato, plus a whole chicken," he said. "And then, only a few hours after, dinner. Five courses from the dining room. She ate it all the nurse reported. ALL. In one sitting."

"But how can that be allowed? What do the doctors say?"

He shrugged. "No matter what they say. There's nothing anyone can do."

"They say it will be sent up," she told Maggie when she reentered her room.

(I'd be a little careful and not eat all of it, she thought she should have added.) Goodbye, Maggie and take care. I'll do a healing drawing for you—she had come to believe drawings could heal. She thought she should have added all that, too. But as she turned to leave, she only nodded and waved, stupidly murmuring, "Get rest."

The tiny terrace of her own small room faced the Duomo which oppressed her. Much of Florence oppressed her, if not the art works or those they depicted—Venus, the Three Graces, the Davids—its narrow streets, its stone, so punishing to the legs and feet. Some of the shrill voices. "Madam," one had said to her after she had sipped another lemon drink—those delicious limones!—and then put the paper cup, when she had finished, down on the stone steps. "Madam, this is not the trash." (Trashcans she was told could be found on every corner though she stood on a corner and saw none.) No, Florence was certainly not "the trash." The art sometimes stopped breath, yes that was true, the architecture, too. And even the Arno—which in photographs had looked ugly to her—a dirty brown—was, when she actually looked into it, clear. But Florence was also now to her, punishing. A punishing city. Overcrowded with tourists. In September, yes. And, yes, with menace. Even with art. ("At this point I don't give a shit who it's by," she had heard an exhausted tourist say to his guide in one of the galleries.) Over crowded, claustrophobic and hard.

And expensive. She realized when she paid for her own dinner that evening that her funds were dwindling, her pensionne twice the price of the room she had in Rome and not nearly as spacious. She wasn't sure she could comfortably go on to the north and east without somehow acquiring more money. Maybe if she went back to the south she could sell some sketches? She had seen artists selling their work in the Piazza Navona, and even a few sketching (amateurs they seemed to be, some of them American) not far from the Colosseum and Forum.

Never mind how much she thought she should get to Padua. Would it be ungrateful of her to put that trip off? Maybe her encounter with Maggie had simply unnerved her? Presented her with a test? In her dream San Antonio of Padua had directed her and San Antonio of Sorrento had said, "Keep a straight course." She wanted to please them. Let them direct her. Childlike, she told herself, or rather, childish! (Yes, yes, I know.) And yet, somehow, I must.

But not long after she got on the train going east, (a bend she had to admit in her "course") it stopped. Stopped for a long time and then began to back track. And only after it started backtracking did she hear from some young women, Americans tourists like herself, that a train on an opposite track had caught fire. When she looked out the window the blue sky had turned red, gave off a dark pink glow. She could hear a chopping noise, and then out her window see the helicopters landing. Her train, the women told her, would have to back track all the way to Florence and then they would have to re-board a train on another track.

When that finally happened, the train she boarded was bound for Rome where she imagined she had left her heart.

She had tried to stay on a straight course, but maybe Sorrento to Rome was the straight course and she had left it. Maybe a back track now was intended. She didn't know. She only knew that the direction in which she was now traveling—which she alone had chosen after she found herself again in the once medieval city—felt right.

Chapter 8

*A*nd made her happy. Space and sunshine. This sweet life! And the best pasta she had ever tasted! With shellfish and a cream sauce. She had hardly begun to enjoy it when the proprietor of the little restaurante, on a side street not far from the Colosseum, where she was taking her dinner, walked over to her and said, "If you would be so kind, I've something to ask."

"Of course," she answered, instantly mesmerized by his presence, this stocky little man with kind eyes and receding hair.

"A week or so ago I observed you sketching some of the trees. When I walked by, you didn't seem to notice—but I saw the picture you were making and some others in your sketch book which you had left behind you on the stone wall."

"Oh," she caught her breath, "did you?"

"Fresh," he said. "So simple. Beautiful. As a child would draw a tree." He smiled when he saw her flinch. "A child, of course, with a gift." He paused. "I wonder—am wondering—do you have any for sale?" He motioned toward the bare space on the walls of his plain little dining room." I would like—I need—pictures—and I like yours—those I saw—The trees. Some believe they have spirits—do you feel that?—perhaps, as you draw?''

She smiled, aware for the first time of what had brought her back. "Yes," she said. "I didn't realize it until now—but I believe I do."

"As a child would draw them." That is what Mario had said (he told her to call him "Mario"). And, she told herself, when drawing first came back to me (and it was here!) I had reprimanded myself for my lack of skill—for drawing the parasol pines as a child would draw them. She remembered then the story of San Antonio—that when, on request of the pope, he was visiting a wealthy lord and prayed late into a starless night, Jesus appeared to him as a child—as a baby!—(his dark room all at once flooded with brightness) and that forever after he was depicted holding the Christ child who is sitting on his precious book—the one that had been lost.

He was a young man himself, only thirty-six years old when he died. All the little statues she had ever seen of him depicted a slender young person with a sweet face—a kind of boy-brother to the small sacred one forever sitting on the beloved word of his book.

Though Rome is a city of stone, she told herself as she took out her colored pencils, I have come back to draw the trees.

It was such a pleasure—and so easy—to pencil their likeness. Maybe something of their essence, even, on paper. Did they have spirits? Just a short while before she had heard herself say she thought they did. Was the earth she stood on, and all that sprung from it, inhabited? Did she have some early Christian or even pre Christian memory in her genes? And did that, along, of course, with her beloved saints, direct her?

"It's all inhabited," she heard one of the tourists who passed her as she worked at the larger sketches she was now making for the restaurant, propped up on her easel. "The Colosseum, the Forum—the whole place. I've been here lots of times. I can always feel it—" And then, "What are you drawing there? —Oh, I see. The pines."

"Yes," Beatrice told her, "and I have at least once been asked if I believe there are spirits in these trees." As she spoke she felt the midday September sun beat down upon her, saw the sky above her as no longer blue but pink, and she realized suddenly that she was really hot. "I will do others," she said, "This one is for the little restaurante—" and then she pointed toward it. "A place down that street, there." The top of the small tree she sketched, an umbrella that might have sheltered a child who could have been Frannie's—or her own if she had had a child—or the Christ Child, Himself—that Love, that pure, pure Love—who she thought, perhaps, lives in all of us somewhere—though sometimes buried deep—almost seemed to speak to her. As the sun beat down hard upon her, how she wished she knew what it wanted to say!

So hot. She had grown up in heat, could deal with heat, she told herself. Now she needed to be under one of these green parasols, not apart from it. But to draw it, of course, she had to be apart.

The large pines, which surrounded the small tree she drew, seemed to smile. Did she see them smile? Her pencil moved quickly, making broad strokes, sketching all the trees sheltering the small one. A circle of trees. Green. Then green emitting a pinkish light. She was drawing, she told herself, surprised, a second sun. A sun that was also a shelter whose every part also seemed to encase a personage, although she didn't know, had no idea about, who any one of them were. Maybe I would know, she told herself, if I were not so hot.

She fell then. And when she came to she was in a bed in a room in which the walls seemed to trap her. Others were also in beds in that room, and one of them, the one that was in the bed across from her was—Maggie!

"You are everywhere," she heard herself say. "Appear everywhere."

Maggie smiled and she thought she heard her say, "We're both fuckin' freaks. Artist and invalid. Shacked up together today."

Chapter 9

She had fallen, Mario told her, probably from standing too long in the sun and had been taken to a hospital where she saw the American woman from the tour, who had returned to Rome for some final days before departure, before she left for the states with the others. They would leave from the Leonardo da Vinci Airport by the end of the week.

"You fainted from too much sun," she heard him repeating.

"No," she said. "The trees are inhabited. I was in a kind of rapture."

"This city," Mario said, winking at her as he hung the pictures, "this city enraptures."

Yes, she told herself, there were shades of babies, of children in those trees. Aloud she said to Mario, "The woman. There she was! And I thought I'd never see her again."

"She has a weak heart," Mario said, "but she's all right now. Soon she will see her own American doctor. You mustn't worry about her. The tour was too much. They had been to Florence, to the lakes, to Venice."

"Venice!" Maggie screamed at her (she sat propped upon pillows on one of the plush couches in the lobby of the Hotel Napoleon where the group was housed their last night in town) "Venice stinks!" She shook an accusing fist then at Beatrice and yelled, "A stinking hole! What a fucking stench! It's rotting. Sinking into that filthy fucking water! It smells like shit."

"But the art—" Bea murmured.

"I never cared about it. Never gave a fucking damn—and it left me half blind. I can only half see now, everything's blurry—the Palace of

San Marco full of shitting birds! And if that wasn't enough, they dragged us to other places."

Bea sucked in her breath. "Padua? Did they take you to Padua?"

"To the freakin' saint!?" Maggie all but screamed out at her. "Nothing left of him but his jaw bone and his freakin' tongue! The nasty thing! On display behind a case! One look and I wanted to throw up—I hate it—I hate Italy!"

After that, their last encounter, Bea often heard herself whispering under her breath, (thinking of her own voice as if it belonged to another person), "San Antonio, please, please, please find—" (Oh, what word to use?)

"Please!" she finally said aloud. "Please help."

Part Two

Chapter 10

Mario bought several of her pictures for a good price and when she told him how grateful she was, that she hadn't known how she could remain in Rome much longer, that she was emotionally exhausted and also running out of funds, he arranged for her to stay—cost free—in a villa across from the Tiber whose owner—his friend—was away for the late summer and autumn months and whose grounds sprouted many trees. Pines, yes, with parasols. She had never before seen so many of such towering height all together in one location, especially surprising in this one—their various groupings and postures suggesting stories. Stories she somehow needed to document on her sketchpad.

The three grouped together across the length of the pool began with what she thought of as a mother tree in the center, positioned very near one somewhat smaller and a little apart from one of even greater height, their placement drawing her to some domestic drama and at the same time bringing to her, the viewer who hoped to capture what their interplay was about, a quieting of the heart. Then she was lost in the color of the tops of the trees and in the magic of Rome's October light, feeling herself drawn to and becoming a part of the blue-green sky.

That night in her huge bedroom under the ceiling that seemed to reach for the sky he was also there—the young preacher—with the face of a teenager, really—who held a book with a babe sitting on it. Both bathed in light and yet a light that was penetrated by the same blue-green azure that she had felt herself lifted into when she had sat poolside and begun to sketch the trees. The light—the purity—(pure love, she told herself, that's what it is) enveloped her. She was not afraid. These two innocents in the light and in the blue-green color wrapped themselves around the walls, moved around the big room in a circular way, so that they were reflected in the gilding and in the mirrors with such an envelopment that in that moment she felt no harm could ever come to her. There they were before and all around her. A child holding a child.

One afternoon the little girl—granddaughter of the Romanian caretaker, who with his wife and daughter-in-law, lived in an apartment adjoining the villa's garage—appeared by the pool where she sketched. She had been trying so hard to capture what she remembered of his sweet face, the young preacher, when she heard the girl laughing and was startled then to hear her say in perfect English, "Good morning. My mother would like to know if we could bring you something. We've made little cakes."

"They sound delicious," she heard herself saying, (for she had felt removed, in another realm, even as she looked at this slender child with brownish red hair)—then even though she had been startled, asking the standard question, "What is your name?"

"Arabella. Don't you think that's a beautiful name?"

She smiled and nodded.

"I'm six years old," Arabella said holding up five fingers on one hand and her thumb on the other. "And I go to school and am learning French as well as how to read Italian."

"And your parents have taught you English?"

"My mother IS English," Arabella said. "Would you like to meet her?

"I would," Bea said.

When Beatrice had arrived at the villa she had only met Nicola, Arabella's young grandfather —she didn't think he was yet fifty. His son, it turned out, had met an English girl (on the Spanish steps) he was quick to marry shortly after his family had moved to Italy, but was now away, back in Romania, finally finishing a university course of study—his wife, Arabella's mother, expecting a second child, a boy Arabella said. "Not another girl," she seemed pleased to report.

How serene, Bea thought, how serene my new life here under the protection of these green trees, how serene my life is becoming and how glad I am to be with this family, caretakers of this villa, these grounds, and this precocious child who doesn't know what to expect, but seems to be peacefully waiting for a brother.

That night in her room, the saint, holding the babe and a book and a single flower—a lily of the field it seemed to be—once again bathed in blue green light, revolved around her walls, figures so large that they extended to and even through her tall ceiling, lifting it—and her, too—into another realm. Then the brown robed young man with the shining face—still holding babe and book and flower—began to speak.

"I had wanted to stay in Morocco from which the bodies of young monks in Lisbon where I had grown up and first studied theology had been returned, but I grew sick there—so sick I had to be sent home, to what was then Spain.

"We had not been at sea long when the storm came up and found us. And the little ship they put me on could not stay on course. The winds blew hard tossing us from side to side, but not front to back which would have cracked our vessel in two and doomed us to the deep."

Doomed us—doomed us to the deep—the words seemed to repeat and repeat and she found herself somehow with him—the sweet young man who had been telling his story—at what she thought of as the top of the world which was also, of course near the top of her gigantic room with its fifteen-foot ceiling. There she was near the Christ child, in the arms of this older—and completely human child, for the tall slender figure with the sweet face looked not much older than a boy.

"Side to side we were thrown!" she heard him say. "I became sicker and sicker—with nausea as well as with my rising fever—finally not caring if I lived, praying—when I could pray at all—only for an end to suffering. I don't know how many days or weeks we were tossed, only that my sickness became my agony."

By his side she felt herself thrown, this way and that, with her own nausea rising and then—

Then she felt in her own arms a child, a girl child—her own—

And, then, felt her child slipping, slipping from her, falling away—

And she awoke.

Crying softly (she had heard no thud), crying in a way that did not hurt (she remembered that sometimes she cried so hard it hurt her throat) because she saw a form before her—so lovely—heard it say, "Mama, Mama. You didn't lose me. I'll always be with you. It's all right."

How could she have forgotten?

It was so deep—this loss. She had remembered the loss of her friend, Frannie, who had left a motherless child in the world.

But not her own loss of one who left her a mother without a child.

She had pushed that loss down even deeper, along with the memory of her child's gentle father, the husband she had loved with the soft lines around his eyes and mouth. She had pushed him away, ordered him away from her. Had withdrawn from his embrace, sobbing and said, nearly chocking on the words as she spit them out, "Please go."

And when he wouldn't, repeated them over and over until a nurse came in and gave her a pill and told him she needed sleep. She remembered how his lips felt on her cheek and how his shoulders drooped when he turned toward the door.

And later—she supposed it was the next day—she remembered someone telling her that he had tried to come back to her, but as he turned, crossing lanes at a dangerous intersection, he had been struck by an oncoming car.

She had not been able to say "good-bye." She had not been able to say, "I love you." And the pain of knowing was so sharp that it cut memory away (memory that held both him and the child they had lost) with one terrible slice.

And now here she was in a room with a myth who had become a presence. Here she was with her legendary San Antonio who had just spoken of his own suffering, of a sickness so painful he could only think of it as martyrdom. But who said, "Like everything else, like life itself, it was finally over."

The ship upon which he had suffered at last drifted toward shore and he was rescued and nursed back to health and his senses by monks who told him he was on the east coast of Sicily. In the same monastery where Francis had also recovered from an illness and where San Antonio (who said nothing of his previous theological training) asked to be instructed in Franciscan life.

What was she to make of it all? What kind of dream—if that was what it had been? Terrible, yes, but also oddly beautiful.

A beautiful simplicity about it.

If also shock.

Like San Antonio, she told herself, and the child he always holds.

And—she hesitated to even think this—her own child. The baby she now remembered who had not lived long after birth.

But also the spirit—a precious spirit (was it —would it perhaps always be—inside her?)—who had just spoken to her and said, "I'm all right."

Chapter 11

Somehow that made her all right, too. And she was no longer distressed, but, curiously, at ease—though lost in what two nights before she had heard and seen. Yes, for a while she had been stunned and then grieved. She had stayed in her room and wept through some of the next day, but then slept long and without dreams and when she woke she remembered more of San Antonio's story, which she had read about a few weeks before in the villa's library, almost as if he, himself, had told it to her.

He had taken the name Anthony after Anthony of Egypt who meditated in caves and in whose memory all monastic orders came forth—a name also taken by San Antonino of Sorrento who may have helped her San Antonio arrive safely in a place where he could receive care from the monks of Sicily's coast. He told them nothing of his instruction in theology and they blessed him with his first choice of assignments, a simple sequestered life in a hermitage in the north. A place he loved, but was not destined to stay.

There at a meal after the ordination of Dominicans and Franciscans he was asked to give a short sermon. "Just something simple," the host said. For he thought Anthony had no education.

And at first Anthony declined. But then, seeing no one else would speak and that someone had to, he began. He wanted to say just a few words that anyone could understand, but which had great meaning—then realized that only his Lord had the gift to do that—and as he went on, he became excited and drew more and more upon his learning. And his history was exposed.

He was told he must be a public preacher and when the news reached Francis, his senior by thirteen years—beloved by all—Francis gave Anthony an assignment in the north.

But there not everyone listened. And when that happened he went to the river. And when he spoke of love, of forgiveness, the fishes jumped! Glittering in the sun—the blue of them flashing. The blue-green. The amber. The silver! (How she wished she could paint that!) Some so near that when he reached out to touch them they caressed his hand. And when those who had not been listening saw this, they drew nearer and Anthony's friends, the fishes, to listen.

After this he became a preaching traveler who journeyed all over northern Italy and into France. Not, he said, to chastise those who didn't believe or for their transgressions, but to speak of joy, of love.

Of connectedness with all its miraculous wonders.

When some time passed Francis, who had been skeptical of learned teachers, nevertheless, made Anthony one—but gave him warning not to become puffed up. And Anthony served happily and humbly for many years, grateful for friendships he made and hours he could spend with his beloved book. The psalms were in it and pages upon which he could write.

Then one day he found it missing. He had never felt such loss and prayed and prayed it would be found. Shortly after, a young novice who had left the order came back, penitent, and with Anthony's beloved book in his hand!

Anthony's work in the order always made him glad. Most of it in Padua, but sometimes Francis asked him to travel to visit certain lords, and one night when he was away on such a visit and praying in his room a brilliant light filled it.

And he later reported in a soft voice, nearly a whisper "My lord appeared to me then—such a wonder—in the form of a little child."

Then his health began to fail and he traveled to Rome to ask to be freed from duties and, for a time, he was. But then was recalled to Rome and sent back north to preach Lenten sermons and so many came to hear them that he had to speak outside of town centers in open fields, some filled with lilies, some with other wildflowers and there, after also hearing many confessions and other personal stories, he became exhausted and all his energy slipped from him.

He tried to travel through the fields back to Padua, but he had to stop in a small village where he received the sacrament and prayed with the friars, blessing Padua from there.

Then he had a vision and when those with him asked why he was staring, he whispered, "I see my Lord."

And, afterwards, took his last breath.

That morning as she remembered the story of the same San Antonio who had (seemingly) spoken to her so personally just two nights before —and who had given her memory back to her—she went to the drawing room of the villa and again pulled one of the beautifully illustrated books with large prints of the saints from the shelves, one of them by Bellini of Saint Francis receiving the wounds in his hands of Christ, a slant-eyed donkey nearby—and even a small one of San Antonio, described as a "minor friar," but also as "a marvelous vessel of the Holy Ghost," for people who spoke different languages could understand a sermon he preached just as they had, according to biblical account, at the time of Pentecost.

In the picture he was holding a book, undoubtedly the book of psalms he loved so much, but which had been stolen from him, and then returned by the one who took it and who asked forgiveness. He also held a radiant baby like the one who had circled him in a guest room (just as he had circled hers, she thought!), as well as a lily, a flower of the field where he had preached.

Looking at the picture made her want to draw her own.

San Antonio standing in a field of wildflowers. Or, she considered, simply standing on a plot of ground under a tall tree, a thought that took her with her sketch pad out under the pines, poolside, where she began to draw. A sweet young man's face. Then the outlines of a slender body under long brown robes, a babe supported by a book and cradled by one robed arm, the other arm lifted, seeming almost to hold the tree trunk as the handle of a parasol, its protective greenery draped (and sparkling) above him.

"The man in your picture is too warm. He must want to shade himself from the sun."

Arabella had suddenly appeared beside her. "That's why he has an umbrella."

Bea dropped her drawing pencil. "Arabella, where did you come from? I thought you were in school today."

"Mummy let me stay here. I didn't feel well when I woke up. But I'm better now. Who is the man in your picture?"

"A saint of the church who lived long ago—hundreds and hundreds of years ago—who died young. One day in school you may learn more about him." Bea had found out that Arabella went to Catholic school from Arabella's grandfather who spoke very little English but was learning through tapes his son sent and that he often listened to through a headset that he wore when he was walking or doing work on the grounds.

"Is that his baby?" Arabella touched the drawing paper and placed her finger on a fat fist.

"It's baby Jesus," Bea said, "who he loved."

"Do you think I will love Mummy's new baby? Do you like babies?" Arabella dropped her hand from the picture and shifted her weight from side to side.

Bea shrugged, but would not let herself take in the question. "I haven't been around many babies,"—she paused trying not to remember—"but I think your brother will be a baby I could like—and,"—she paused again—"do you know why?"

"Why?" Arabella, who looked much younger than she had when they first met only a few days before, asked and touched Bea's picture with one hand. "Why do you think so?"

"Because," Bea told her as she tore off a piece of her drawing paper from a large tablet and handed it to her, "because he will be at least a little like you."

Chapter 12

As she went on sketching and the days grew short she could not move the hand with which she drew fast enough to trace the features of all who appeared in her mind's eye—San Antonio, again and again, yes, but also mothers and fathers and children whose faces came to her as she looked up through the green of the trees—no , she couldn't remember the tiny face of the child she had lost—and the grief that had erased memory, plus the awfulness that had enveloped her from the afflicted, inescapable Maggie, ceased.

Some of the figures she saw in the trees were playful—and seemed loving—but there came a time when a few seemed to menace and, on the first cool autumnal afternoon, in one she thought she saw Maggie's face!

Then a few nights later that face came back in a dream and it WAS Maggie's and bore down upon her so that Bea swirled away from it and out of her bed where, standing firmly on her feet, she asked, "What do you want of me?"

And she thought she heard Maggie whisper something. And when that perception returned, clearly heard her say, "Set me free."

The next day she began to draw not only the trees, but the figures of all those she imagined she had lost beneath them. There was the lost boy —the first love of her youth who had been orphaned by a plane crash (did that foreshadow her husband's death?), then her friend who had been killed in a war—for a moment she couldn't remember which one, there had been so many— then her mother who had died so long ago and left her with relatives, luckily, kind ones (she had been a child, younger even than Arabella). And finally, a large figure of a woman with Maggie's pleading face.

How was it that she had put that down on her drawing paper? She hardly knew how she had done it—but there it was looking back at her—and in her head she once again heard Maggie's plea. Then, fully conscious of what she was about, she began to make more sketches of her. And one, at last, in which she looked a little sad, but less deranged.

Then she saw what she with her last strokes, without meaning to, had done.

"Oh, I don't know how," she said aloud. "I don't know how—" She was almost screaming it.

She had twisted the mouth on that face, turned the lines of it. Saw that she had done it. No, she told herself, I didn't mean to, I didn't mean to.

She had wanted to draw a face that was composed.

That night in her bedroom with the seemingly unreachable ceiling, just before she drifted off into a restless sleep, she once again saw the figure of the saint circling the walls of her room. "San Antonio," she heard herself say, "Please find a way to help me—to help ME! (She seemed stuck on the word.) And to also, somehow, set Maggie free."

Chapter 13

By the time she woke she felt almost herself again. And she shook off that request. Shook off her visions.

No—no—Maggie, she was sure San Antonio would tell her if he could, had to somehow free herself, and she thought even he would be hard-pressed to find a way for her to do it.

She remembered then an angrier than usual Maggie telling her she would not send her grandchildren, "those ugly brats whose mother thinks I am a freakin' checkbook," Christmas gifts. Instead she said she would send a card saying she'd given to the Smile Train and let them make what they would of that.

No. No more sketches of Maggie, she told herself. When I go down to the pool to draw I will simply sketch more of the grounds, the pool, the trees. When she reached her sketching site pool side she saw Arabella in the water, swimming beneath it, her gray bathing suit flickering silver as if she were—as she had so often heard Mother's say of children in swimming suits like these—part fish. Arabella seemed to be missing yet another school day, this one with a little late October chill in the air. That water, Bea thought, must be cold.

"Aren't you freezing?" she asked Arabella as she emerged.

"No," Arabella said, smiling as she moved toward her "after the first plunge, it's fine. What are you drawing?" She was, Bea noticed, looking down at the drawing pad with Maggie's tormented face on it. "Who is the lady?"

"Someone I met when I was touring," Bea said. "A woman who wasn't well—who—" she hesitated—"who was all alone and couldn't be happy."

"You're alone," Arabella said.

Bea laughed. "How can you say that? Here I am under the protection of all these—" she paused, "inhabited trees. I sketch faces in their branches! And—" she paused again, "this morning I'm here with you."

Arabella smiled a little. "Will you draw more pictures of the woman today?"

Bea shook her head. "No."

"I like the pictures you make of the trees—the faces you put in them" She pointed to Bea's sketch pad. "In this one there seems to be a mother, a father, and—"

"Arabella," Bea said, interrupting her, "Why aren't you in school today?"

Arabella dropped her head. "I felt sick again this morning."

"But better now?"

"Oh yes." She lifted her head and looked up at Bea and then past her to the trees.

"Do you know what," Bea said, "this morning I don't think I will any more sketch the trees at all. If you'll agree to stand more or less still for a little while, I think I'd like to sketch YOU."

And so, Beatrice began to draw a series of sketches of a radiant girl child.

"Let's keep this a secret," Arabella said.

"Why a secret?" Bea asked as the October light illuminated Arabella and the spot where she stood in such a way that truly seemed to make impossible keeping anything about either her or the pictures Bea had sketched of her a secret.

"Well," Arabella said, "I've been thinking—that, maybe, I could have one—to give as a present."

"Of course," Bea said "For Christmas? Or a birthday?"

"Maybe both," Arabella said. "I've saved a little of the money Mummy gives me. I could pay you something for it."

Then Bea remembered Arabella's brother would be born in December. "For your mother, who has given me so many sweets?" she asked and then added with a smile, "I wouldn't let you pay me anything for it."

"For my father, too—" Her lip trembled a little. "He'll be back Mummy says, in December."

"You'll be glad to see him, won't you?"

Arabella smiled and nodded. She had, Bea thought, before this been about to cry. "Between now and December we'll do a lot more pictures on weekends—and when you come home from school—you should try not to miss many more days, you know—and I'm sure they will make your father very happy. And do you know what?"

"What?" Arabella asked.

"I think just maybe your baby brother should have one."

Arabella laughed. "He wouldn't know what it was. He'll be a baby. I've seen babies. Babies don't know anything."

"Well, not for a while," Bea said as she watched the irrepressible Arabella jump up and down, "but one day he will know it's from his smart, ENERGETIC—talented—and very generous—older sister. And that she gave it to him when he was born."

As time passed Bea met Arabella every Saturday morning and made many sketches of her. Often with the command, "Keep still!" Arabella's mother by this time confined to bed, for she had once been in danger of losing her child, and her father-in-law, Arabella's grandfather, often away on the other side of their living quarters, overseeing the villa's grounds while his wife spent much of her day moving between the kitchen and her daughter-in-law's room, enabling Bea and Arabella to keep their secret bond.

"I just tell Mummy I'm going to visit you by the pool," Arabella whispered the first day she appeared. "She told me not to bother you as you drew and that she's sorry she can't anymore make and give you her special cakes."

After their third session they began to draw up together a list of gifts they planned to give over the holidays, sketches of Arabella for Mother, Father, and possibly, Brother at the top of the list. When it became too chilly for her to swim Arabella with some instruction took to sketching, too, and, as with everything Bea had ever seen her do—from swimming to speaking French—she excelled from the start. She sketched the pool and yes, the group of pines that Bea had so often seen in terms of family—mother near daughter—father, large, and seemingly protective, but also somewhat apart. "You should give one of your own pictures to your mother and father," Bea suggested. "Several of them, maybe."

"Who will you give your pictures to?" Arabella asked. "Besides the ones of me I mean."

Bea shrugged, then said, "Perhaps I'll give one to Mario—your father's friend who arranged for me to stay here and who is now arranging for me to have a space to sell my pictures in the Piazza Navona."

"And the sad lady you tried to draw—" She pointed to the sketch of Maggie with the twisted mouth. "Won't you send her a picture?"

"No," Bea said, "I don't have anything she would like. She doesn't really like pictures." She remembered Maggie's reaction to the book she'd bought at the Uffizi filled with shots of Giottos, Raphaels, Botticellis, Leonardos. "I never gave a freakin' damn about seeing anything in that place." The way she threw the book with photos of many paintings aside and demanded pizza and gelatos for dinner. "She doesn't really like pictures. Not even great ones. Besides, I don't believe I have her address."

But Mario did have it she found out the evening when she crossed the Tiber into Rome to see him and to have the creamy pasta she liked so much with her favorite red wine.

"Yes," he said, "I put it in my book after I went to the hospital to see you. And there they told me that you had been on the tour together, that she was your friend."

"I don't know why I asked," Bea said. "She wasn't really my friend."

"You have, "Mario said, "taken on her pain."

She was in a neutral place after that.

She had wanted to scream, "I didn't mean to!" Screamed it in her mind, but couldn't project any sound when she opened her mouth to cry out.

Arabella continued to pose for her on Saturday mornings under the trees. And to sketch them with her sometimes, too. But a few Saturdays they had to miss for some rains came in November and more early in December and on a number of Saturdays then Bea stayed in her room where at night she was no longer enveloped in visions, sometimes sketching the furnishings and what she saw before her on the walls, the ten foot gilded mirror to the left of her giant bed, the window, almost of the same length to her right, rain slashing against it. Then one night after the rain was done, a fantastic star.

Its light seemed to circle the walls of the villa and extend toward what she thought of as a blessed family of trees—those that sheltered her and Arabella as they made pictures near the pool where they first had met.

The morning after she saw it, she walked across the soggy grounds to draw, wet earth or no, and when she turned to take her sketchpad from the satchel she had placed on a damp chair, she saw Arabella skipping toward her and shouting, "My father is coming home!" Then Grandfather Nicola approached, wearing his headset. "Anglish," he said, tapping his earphones and smiling, then handing her a letter. "From," he said, "the United States."

Chapter 14

The postmark she saw was Ohio, but the handwriting was not Maggie's bold one. For a moment she thought it must instead be from Maggie's daughter. Maybe Maggie was gravely ill or even dead.

But, no, the letter was, instead, from Maggie's granddaughter, Margaret, who explained that her mother had obtained an address where a message might reach her. Someone had written it on the inside cover of a book from the Uffizi gallery in Florence—it didn't look like her grandmother's handwriting she said. "I'm glad to have it," she went on, "because I'm soon coming to

Rome. A semester abroad! My mother had ALL of her junior year in Paris when she was in college and she's told me so many wonderful stories about it. I want to spend most of my time in Rome, though," she went on "because I'm particularly interested in the Baroque. The richness of it, the flamboyance." She hoped Beatrice was still there and would remain for a while and that they could at least meet.

Arabella's mother had, in fact, just a day or two before, asked Bea to stay on until at least the summer. The owner who was now in South Africa would not be back for perhaps another year. Arabella would benefit from her company when she would be occupied with the new baby. Since Beatrice and Arabella had been spending time together Arabella was much more cheerful. "I couldn't help but notice," her mother said, "her drawing—some of it quite good, I think. She doesn't complain in the mornings that she's unwell ... You know my pregnancy has been hard on her, too—and she has more than just missed her father. But we're going have him back—and in just a few weeks."

Bea, who had no memory of her own father —he had, her mother said. simply disappeared, out of work, sick, despondent—and who often had a hard time meeting new people now felt obligated to welcome two into her life.

She would have known her even if she had not been told what she would be wearing or that she would be standing in front of the Bernini fountain of the Four Rivers in the Piazza Navona. She looked so all-American—and never mind that it was December—so Fourth-of-July.

If Maggie had been young, smiling and still on the slender side, she would have looked just like this attractive girl, her granddaughter, all in blue, a navy flared jacket above her wide matching skirt, navy pumps, and on her dark brown head, as she moved it, a little navy cap tilted to one side—a bobbling ivory flower!

Named for Maggie and if never the recipient of a Christmas gift, she had at least claimed the gift book Beatrice had bought in the Uffizi—on a page of which Mario when visiting at the hospital had scribbled Bea's address. And in Rome at this Christmas season she held it in her hands.

"Your grandmother gave the book to you?" Bea's first question after she said, "Margaret, I'm Beatrice," and reached out for an embrace.

The girl only laughed. But later when she and Bea had moved to one of the nearby restaurants and they were seated at a sunny outdoor table she said, "My grandmother has never been a giver, but when she saw I was interested in the book—I spied it on top of her luggage in a corner of the room—she said, 'Take it. I don't give a freakin' damn about the fucking thing!'" Then she paused and said, "Sorry. But I expect you know she talks that way."

Bea smiled then asked, "How is she?"

The girl winced, and fingered pages of the book she still held in one hand. "The doctor keeps her drugged. He's given her an appetite suppressant. She's not in so much pain now. Though, God forbid, those of us around her know that." Her voice dropped. "We don't know how long she can last. She has become a little easier to be around—a little more accepting." She paused and smiled, flipping the book open, "One day she might even pay tribute to the Three Graces or even to Venus herself in one of these Botticelli's."

"You've come to study art then," Beatrice said.

"Art history. Antioch will give credit. I came early because I got a low fare and because I thought it would be special to tour the Vatican Museums and St. Peters at Christmas—to be here for all the festivities. Something I can write a paper about—and that I've always wanted to do—and, no, I'm not Catholic. No one in my family is even church going anymore—though they once went to the Presbyterian. You're a painter, aren't you?"

"No. No—well, once I painted a little. Now I only sketch—draw with colored pencils." She paused. "For a long time, you see, I lost my ability to use any medium. When I was young I had a modest gift, but then, somehow, I lost it. Here, although my drawings are simple, a little of it has come back to me. And my friend, Mario, who I believe wrote my address in your book has arranged for me to have a space here." She pointed toward the far end of the piazza, much of which had been transformed into a Christmas market. "It's practically in the street—but maybe that means the first of the tourists will stop—or some of them—" She paused. "And Margaret, about painting and sculpture, too, you'll have to educate me. I've always drawn—well, except for that time when something happened that stopped me—but I've forgotten much of what I knew about Art History. We'll have to do some viewing together— that is, if you won't mind. I'd like to go with you sometime to the Vatican museums, or to the Borghese. Of course, in Rome, it's everywhere, isn't it? In the street, in all the piazzas."

"Yes. Oh yes. I look forward to seeing what I can and I'd be happy for you to come with me to all the viewing places. I guess you can live here for years and years and not see everything."

This girl, so composed, so seemingly sure of herself, and much older than twenty, suddenly struck her as someone she'd been waiting to know all her life.

"When I was a child," Bea told her, "I would sometimes lose my drawing pencils—and then, when I grew up, I lost a beloved art teacher—the only good one I had. Also many friends—" She stopped, wondering if she should go on. "And later, Margaret, I lost a child who died shortly after birth." She stopped again. She hadn't meant to become so Confessional. "And then," she continued, "her father was killed in an auto accident. So terrible a thing I even lost the memory of it."

The wine arrived. Just in time! Bea thought. Then the pasta. The two women clicked glasses.

"But you got it back?"

Beatrice nodded.

"How did that happen?"

"Well," Bea said, "I do believe partially through a saint." She paused. "Maybe you know about him—Saint Anthony—the Finder."

"Are you Catholic?"

"No—but when I was very young I had a friend who was."

"And she told you about the saints?"

Beatrice laughed. The wine had warmed her and she took several more big swallows. "Not all, but some of them—a little. And when I grew up—was in fact, in middle life, I had another friend who told me more."

"Well, then," Margaret said, twirling her pasta, "you should give them a nod now and then in your drawing."

"Of course," Bea said to herself as well as to Margaret. "Faces in my trees." Then she laughed. "You see when I began to draw again—and for a long time I didn't draw at all—mostly I just drew trees. They seemed special to me here. Inhabited. And so I drew faces in some of them. Family groupings—or so they seemed to me. Then, not long ago, I stopped and just began to sketch the little girl who lives with her English mother and Romanian grandparents, the caretakers of the villa where I live—her mother expecting another child—and very soon—her father finishing his Business degree in Romania and on his way back to them."

She stopped and took another sip of wine. "All of them far from the saints I'm afraid. And I don't know why I'm telling you any of this—really I want to know more about you—how you became interested in Art History, that is, if you know—and how I can help you get settled."

"No, please," the girl said, "I'm already more or less settled. The college arranged things. And I'm fascinated. Tell me more about the connection with the saints."

"Well," Bea said, "—and I will make an end to my saga here—Several nights in the villa I seemed to see one of them. St. Anthony. Larger than life. So tall he stretched to the ceiling—and then circled my room!"

Margaret put down her fork and her mouth flew open. "Were you asleep?"

"Yes. In retrospect I suppose I was," Beatrice said. "Dreams are, of course, visual. But what I saw was not a visual from an ordinary dream."

Chapter 15

On Margaret's first visit to Beatrice she met the family—Grandfather Nicola, Grandmother Lyset; Mother, Catherine, and Father, Michael, a small, slender, sandy haired man who Lyset said was a talented pianist, but had felt obliged to get his degree in something more practical. And even baby brother, pink-cheeked and as robust as any of the cupids in local galleries ("He looks like my father," Catherine explained.) Arabella—in spite of her displayed gifts—the drawings she had wrapped in silver paper—looked stricken beside him, her mouth turned down at the corners, and, uncharacteristically, stood stock still. But she managed a smile when Bea took a picture of the family scene in the living room of their apartment adjoining the villa's garage. It helped, yes, that it was Christmas—extra special food —Grandmother's baking—a crèche in one corner complete with babe in the manger, Mary and Joseph, shepherds and sheep and other farm animals and overall, hung from a tree branch, a shiny paper star. That made Bea remember the real one—Venus, probably—that only a few nights before she had seen from the tall window in her room. Such a complete celebration! But why not, she asked herself. After all, the first celebration of Christmas was here in Rome, the first mass, she had been told, said in the church of Santa Maria Maggiore, not far from which she had bought a gelato and then gotten lost.

"The lady with the sad face is the new lady's grandmother?" Arabella asked—astonished—when she and Beatrice went into the kitchen together to bring out another tray of Grandmother's sweets and Beatrice whispered, "Yes."

"But she's grown-up," Arabella protested. "I've never thought of grown-ups as having grandmothers."

"Many are lucky," Bea told her. "Many do."

"But then," Arabella said, "then the lady shouldn't be sad. She isn't all alone. You said she was all alone."

"She was when I met her," Bea said. "And even though she now lives with her daughter and granddaughter she's often locked up within herself and they can't reach her or she them."

Arabella laughed. "But that's silly."

"I know it sounds silly—ridiculous," Bea told her. "Because they live together. But, believe me, there are many people in the world who are so sad or angry or just hurt in a way that won't heal that they can't free themselves of the pain to even notice those nearby, much less enjoy them—have fun with them." She smiled. "They've lost a way to do that."

When they rejoined the others Arabella's pale father was at the piano. He didn't look at all as Bea had pictured him, but he played as if he really was the man she had imagined. In charge. Commanding. He had, after all, wanted to major in Music, not Accounting. She and Arabella immediately put down their trays on a nearby table and with the others—Margaret, Arabella's Mother, Catherine; Grandmother Lyset; Grandfather Nicola— and began to sing.

"Bella sera, Bella sera." After they had said these goodnights, Bea took Margaret into the villa's front living room—the villa boasted two living rooms, a rose, and down some stairs, and adjoining a recreation room, a green—and then into a library where she pulled the book of saints in which she had read more extensively about Saint Anthony than she had from the first book upstairs from a shelf full of books about "holy people," along with many atlases, geographies and histories.

"I could spend days in here," Bea said and then pointed to the back wall. "The art histories are back there. Maybe some you'd like to look at. Your grandmother told me that when she was home all she did was read—that she liked to read all day. In bed with the curtains closed."

Margaret laughed, then grew somber and said, "She told you the truth about that."

"Tell me," Bea said, "What did she read?"

"Some books that have to do with psychology—you see, she once aspired to be an analyst." Then Margaret laughed again and said, "These days, mostly she reads romances." After a reflective moment, she added, "That would be funny if it weren't so sad. My grandfather married her for her family's money—and she knew it—and he came to treat her badly—And she needed more than most of us to be loved."

Bea was silent for a moment. Maggie couldn't love herself, she thought, because no one else had. "That's insightful," she said as she sat down in a small gilded chair next to a desk. "And kind of you to say because I gather you were not close."

"No," Margaret told her, "but I was—and am—close to my mother who has helped me understand my grandmother—who was cruel to me when I was very young. I looked like her, you see."

When she caught her breath Bea said, "But you're very—" She hesitated. "Pretty."

"Thank you," Margaret said as she steadied herself against the bookcase. "The day I left to come here my grandmother, who was in the living room as I was about to step out of it, said, 'You look attractive today.' And I said, 'Thank you, Grandmother. I've been told I look like you.' She didn't respond, but my mother who could see us both from the door—my mother told me that she smiled."

Beatrice found it hard to speak, but after some silence said, "Margaret, as you have discovered, here I have become one of Arabella's teachers. I haven't known you long—but it's becoming clear to me already—that I learn from you."

Chapter 16

Maggie's family made its fortune from steel, her father an executive in Pittsburgh with many shares of stock and seldom at home. Her mother, who in her 40s had a difficult time with her daughter's birth and in poor health after, was dead before Maggie was two and Maggie was sent to Youngstown to live with her maternal aunt, a widowed club woman, none too anxious to receive her. But who compensated for her lack of interest and attention by filling Maggie full of sweets, after and even in between every meal. Maggie had a weight problem very early in her young life and was also, with one ailment or another, frequently ill.

After she was old enough to attend school she was often too sick to go and spent weeks of every winter in her bedroom's Princess Bed (especially designed and made for her by a local craftsman) reading library books, mysteries written for young readers and romantic fairy stories, attended by a housekeeper who frequently fluffed her pillows and smoothed her sheets. And who also sometimes read aloud to her after bringing her demitasse cups filled with hot chocolate. "She loves sweets so," the housekeeper sometimes told her aunt when she returned the cups to the kitchen, "I thought—though dinner is not far away—it wouldn't hurt to bring her just a little."

Maggie's aunt shrugged. "All children love sweets," she said. "I'm not concerned about my sister's child eating them." She was, however, beginning to worry that Maggie was becoming anti-social, too withdrawn to speak to anyone in the outside world even by telephone. As a result she encouraged her to use the family phone to order ice cream from the corner drug store that delivered. A practice that erased Maggie's fear of speaking to a strangers and that, along with the treats it brought her, she indulged in frequently and came to enjoy.

Because Maggie missed so much school, her aunt finally hired a tutor for her and then, several, and eventually she was completely educated at home by credentialed teachers the family hired to instruct her. Never far from her bedside (on good days an alcove adjoining her bedroom served as a school room) and often in it.

Doctors, as well as teachers, were frequently summoned to attend to her there and eventually her aunt even arranged for a psychologist to speak with her several times a week. She liked the one that was sent, an attractive young man with a gentle manner—had, the housekeeper said, a little crush on him. Margaret's bed, she also remarked, was not only a place of comfort—and pleasure—but one of power. As long as she was in it, the world—or at least what she desired from it—would come to her. She used the telephone, now installed by her bed, to reach it with her requests, ordering treats from the drug store, and, as time went on, books from a local book store.

By the time Maggie was eighteen she was considered well enough to attend a non-threatening institution of higher learning and was enrolled in a small girl's school in the southern part of the state where she declared an interest in psychology and was permitted to study it in the school's "House Plan" —classes conducted in the dormitory in a central room near student bedrooms; some even came to morning classes in pajamas, a habit that was natural for Maggie to acquire. Maggie was a practiced reader and she quickly also became a learner. With the help of several tutors she did exceptionally well, earning her degree in less than four years.

After that her aunt thought no time should be wasted. Maggie should marry.

But just how her grandfather was persuaded to marry her grandmother, Margaret said was something of a mystery that no one spoke of much. He was from Pittsburgh and of a family of modest means. But he was bright, hardworking and ambitious. A friend of Maggie's aunt had introduced them and it was thought—whispered by some—a deal was struck. A job and a future offered for his willingness to take her grandmother on. And, although he eventually did, he did so reluctantly and then buried himself in his work for the industry and was often away.

"After my mother's birth," Margaret said, "they grew even farther apart. At one point Grandmother considered going to graduate school

—she had surprised herself by doing so well in her college—but she never got there. Never took to motherhood either. My mother was neglected by her, but fortunately, had a loving nannie. And Grandmother wrote and gave checks that weren't asked for even into mother's adulthood. And then complained that she drained her resources for my sister and me and that we only tolerated her presence because she gave us money.

"We hardly knew our grandfather—he was infrequently around—but usually present at holidays. One Christmas I remember him snarling at Grandmother, her head bent over the table where all of us were eating as she spooned heavy whipping cream over a piece of cake (probably at least a second helping) on a large oblong silver plate.

"'A hog at the trough has more restraint,' he whispered as he passed her. But loud enough for all of us to hear."

Chapter 17

The only thing her grandmother had ever given her was a stuffed animal, "a pig," Margaret said, "who wore one of my baby dresses that had my name, Margaret, embroidered on one of the pockets."

"Then," Margaret said, "she laughed. She laughed and laughed when she handed it to me. 'Here,' Porky,' she said, 'this is for you.' I was big when I was born, a more than chubby toddler and seriously overweight as a child. Some of the kids in my school had just days before called me 'Porky' and my grandmother heard them.

"My mother had bought me a beautiful new dress, but I wouldn't wear it. And I wouldn't go to my birthday party. My mother had to tell the children who came that I was sick and in bed and that they shouldn't see me.

"I WAS in bed and I WAS SICK—at heart. So what she said was true."

She stopped. Before she began her story she and Beatrice were both silent. They had retreated to the kitchen and sat on stools at the counter sipping a strong orange tea.

"When I stopped crying I threw the pig against a wall—I had torn the pocket off. When my mother came in she held me for a long time and told me that my grandmother did hurtful things because she hurt so much herself and that, of course, what she had said to me wasn't true. But, I'm afraid that didn't help much. And I was truly glad that until just before I came here—when she said I could have her book from the Uffizi—she never gave me anything again."

"But you've found ways to forgive her?" Bea asked.

"Well, as I got older I became happier. I shot up in height and, after our doctor put me on a really easy food plan—limited sweets but many of the fruits I had always loved—I slimmed down. (I had never been a foodaholic like my grandmother.) My mother and older sister took me shopping. My mother had always kept up with fashion and she and my sister both loved beautiful fabrics and well-made clothes—my sister has become a designer—and they saw to it that I had some. And in the summers when I was a teenager we went on trips. Chicago. And then New York. And in the galleries we visited—the Chicago Art Institute, the Met in New York—I became interested in art. A lot of fleshy gals in some of those paintings!" She laughed. "Wrote about it in my high school newspaper. And began to think I would like to major in it when I went to college. I had always been a pretty good student and in high school I also made friends. Even attracted interest and had a few dates with a boy or two." She stopped to take a breath and another sip of tea. "So life got better. And, of course, I also began to understand that my grandmother was sick. Physically sick. And emotionally, too."

"You began to find your way," Bea said.

Margaret smiled and raised her cup. "Maybe it is the Christ child who is the Finder." She paused. "Anyway, here it is. Christmas. In Italy—and all over the world."

Epilogue

𝒥n the chilly weeks and months that followed Beatrice and Margaret read and discussed books—even one by Dante (Margaret could translate some of what they looked at in Italian)—and viewed many paintings together. A whole room full of Raphael's at the Vatican. "On the walls, on the ceiling—I think maybe even on the floor—though maybe I'm just remembering a reflection," Bea wrote in a letter to Margaret's mother. "Michelangelo's Pieta in St. Peter's, of course—several times—and all the Baroque fountains—the Bernini where we met has become a favorite meeting place. And his wonderful sculpture in the Borghese Gallery. The one that seems, as many have remarked, not so much of stone, but of air."

Then she went on to say that before Easter the two of them decided, with several of Margaret's Art and Art History student friends in the house where she lived and with the approval of its director who also wanted to come along ("the two of us kind of old fashioned chaperons"), to take a mini vacation "in a villa we rented for a week near the end of the Sorrento peninsula right across from Capri—Ischia and Vesuvius in the distance. From our broad terrace we could see all three—and also an old castle that was not far away, its turret shaded by a giant parasol pine.

"One of Margaret's friends who was with us, a little older than the rest, but still a young man—maybe twenty-eight or so—with already thinning hair, a long, thin face and bright brown eyes, a happy twinkle in them, had an ever present smile for us all—but especially for Margaret. She likes him, as she may have told you, and I believe you would, too. A kind man, clearly. (Joy bubbling up in him.) Italian, yes.

"Salvatore Sevini, who waits tables in a restaurant part time. He told us that if he didn't want to one day manage his own gallery, he would aim to be a chef or even a maitre'd. Although we had only bought a few groceries at a local market he took it upon himself to put together our first meal at the villa. Pasta, of course. Then two large (to be shared) perfectly turned out omelets alongside a beautiful fruit dish, followed by a creamy, ("only in Italia") dessert, over which we planned a long day trip to Capri—Anna Capri, in the evening where we hoped to go to a restaurant, which I had once been told is a pinnacle viewing place, to see the moonrise—the most beautiful my friend who has been everywhere said—the most beautiful in the world.

"But then one morning some of us rose early enough to see, instead, from every direction, the afterglow of the sunrise. And the brilliance of it stunned us—the pinks to fuchsias, tangerines to golds. And all of it spilling over that rippling water of so many blues. For a few minutes we were all speechless. Then Margaret said, 'We don't have to go to Capri for a view.'"

"And truly none could be more glorious than what we saw before us—the dusty purple volcano to one side.

"'Certainly it can wait,' Margaret said as we looked down over the water from our hillside terrace at the islands to the little fishing village below and the waves as they slapped against the shore—the light glistening on all their shades of variegated blue.

"'Oh look!' Margaret called out to all of us. Stretching. Raising her arms in the air. 'Just look!'

"All the colors came at us then. Turquoise to azure, all the greens, melons, faint pinks and hot ones. Vermillion and indigo—

"It can wait,'" I said. 'And Heaven, too.'"

Eve La Salle Caram

Eve is the author of five novels, those in her book *Trio, A Corpus Christi Trilogy*, and the interconnected duo of *The Blue Geography* and *Wintershine*. She is also the editor of *Palm Readings, Stories from Southern California*, a multicultural anthology of stories by Southern California women.

For over thirty years she has taught Literature and Writing at California State University, Northridge, and Fiction Writing at UCLA Extension's renowned Writers' Program where she won the Outstanding Instructor in Creative Writing in 2006. She also teaches at Los Angeles City College whose students helped inspire her novel, *Rena, A Late Journey*, and who asked her to write *Looking for Johnny*, the short novel that completes *Trio*. All of her books have been used in Literature and Writing classes in California and in Texas.

With her UCLA Extension Writers' Program colleague and award winning fiction writer and poet, Carolyn Howard Johnson, Eve has conducted writing classes in a villa near the heart of Rome and looks forward to returning to both teach and write.

Please, San Antonio! was inspired by her trips to Italy.

She is grateful to her friends, Mary McFadden Rossetto and Vi Brown, for introducing her to "San Antonio."

In January of 2018, Eve won a Lifetime Achievement Award from *Marquis Who's Who in America*.

Melisande in Paris

Cecilia Manguerra Brainard

Paris 1899

Spring was late that April '99, and Melisande and her Tante Juliette wore heavy woolen coats as they waded through the crowded streets of Paris. They delivered a gown to a client near Notre Dame and bought some sewing notions, after which they waited for a carriage. It took them a good half-an-hour to find one.

Juliette, now cold and impatient, hurriedly lifted herself into the carriage, but both feet had not yet been planted firmly when a large crash spooked the horse—an overloaded crate nearby fell. The horse reared; Juliette teetered and fell. Some men grabbed the horse to keep him from trampling poor Juliette who lay sprawled on the street, her right leg and foot pointing the wrong way. Melisande sucked in her breath and froze, uncertain about what to do. It was Juliette who ordered her to align her own leg the right way.

Meanwhile curious onlookers gathered around them. Two men stepped forward, young and muscular workers with a wagon, who offered to take Juliette to the Hopital Dieu de Paris. "Before you move me," Juliette instructed, "wrap the leg with my coat. It hurts like the devil smashed it ... Be careful ... I'm as fragile as a Sevres. Carefully, my dears, this is how you should carry me."

Melisande walked alongside the wagon and kept a watchful eye on her aunt. The leg was clearly broken. Broken. The gravity of that situation was starting to sink into her. It had taken two men to move her aunt to the wagon. How could she bring her back home with the broken leg? How long would the leg take to heal? And would it heal properly? The father of Etienne, the boy she once loved, fell from the barn and became a cripple. Melisande had heard of amputations of broken limbs that did not heal properly. She was afraid for her aunt.

Juliette on the other hand showed no fear. She smiled and bantered with the men; in fact, she was flirting with them. Juliette was forty-four years old, unmarried, and always looking for her "Romeo," according to Melisande's mother. Juliette was reportedly the least attractive of her five sisters, and to compensate, overdressed, wore loud perfume, and heavy rouge. Juliette reportedly hennaed her mousy-brown hair to keep up with her red-headed sisters. But despite her mother's stories, Melisande found her aunt attractive, like a pretty butterfly, petite, with a nice figure, and full of energy. She worked hard and had made her dress shop popular. Further, she made her own rouge from grapefruit, butter, and beeswax, which sold briskly to her devoted clients. But what impressed Melisande as they hurried to the hospital was Juliette's incredible presence of mind. Had living alone in Paris for decades created this strong independent woman? Melisande's mother had depended on her father for many things.

The waiting room of the Hopital Dieu de Paris had patients with trauma and fractures—people with broken arms, wrists, clavicles, hips, and legs. A construction worker who had fallen off a church roof was immediately whisked to another room. Those with broken wrists and arms sat in chairs; the others, Juliette included, lay on hospital beds. The room smelled of antiseptic. It didn't have a single plant, not a bit of color; it was gray and sad. Melisande was getting depressed, but Juliette kept up her chatter: "that man's nose is as big as a turnip, and that woman is as wide as a door, oh, my goodness, can't they silence that bratty, funny-looking child," and so on. But soon enough, Juliette moaned because her leg was hurting. Melisande peeled back her coat and was shocked to see that Juliette's leg had swelled. She went to the nurse to ask where the doctor was.

The nurse curtly replied that the surgeon was taking care of a man with a broken spine, he would be along, please be patient Mademoiselle, sit down and wait. Melisande was twenty-two, from Lyon, and Parisians intimidated her. Parisians always seemed superior and arrogant—she had heard them say the Lyonnais were only good at making silk and sausages, and while indeed they made excellent silk and sausages, the statement was a put down. Melisande retreated and sat quietly beside her aunt. There they remained for four hours without anything to drink or eat.

(Melisande had offered to buy something, but her aunt didn't want to be left alone.)

It was mid-afternoon when Doctor Samir Martine burst into the room with a brightness that was out of place in that purgatory. He had a broad smile, bouncy walk, and his face was animated as he talked to the nurse. Melisande told her aunt she would talk to him, but the doctor was soon heading toward them. He nodded, eyes fully on Melisande. "Mademoiselle," he greeted, before turning his attention to Juliette who fluttered her eyes when she had a close look of him.

"Madame," he said, "do not worry, you are in good hands. I am the best surgeon in Paris."

Melisande stared at him sharply. In Lyon such braggarts were shunned.

He glanced back at her, their eyes meeting. "Well, no, I am not the best surgeon, but I'm one of the best—" He bent over to uncover Juliette's leg before adding, "—in all of Paris."

Juliette warmed up immediately. "And what is the name of the fine surgeon taking care of me?" She reached up to fuss with her hair, wincing as she did so.

"Doctor Martine," he replied with a flare, sounding like a two-bit actor in a theatrical play; Melisande had to cover her mouth to muffle her laugh.

"How fortunate I am to be helping two beautiful ladies this afternoon. Madame, I have to apply some pressure, you might feel some pain." Juliette gritted her teeth as he pressed the swollen leg at certain points. "Hmmm, some puffiness, but don't worry, everything will be fine."

Before Juliette could say a word, before either of them could react, the doctor held Juliette's leg firmly—huge hands with long fingers, the hands of an artist, Melisande thought—then suddenly, with a quick but precise movement, he pulled apart the bones and snapped them back in place. The ghastly sound made Melisande nauseous. Juliette straightaway fainted.

Unruffled, the doctor ran his hands over her leg. "I had to set her bones before the swelling becomes worse. She'll be fine. Your aunt will have to stay here, you understand, for perhaps two months. If there were no complications, she can go home. She'll need crutches, and she can't put full weight on the leg even after three months."

Melisande's head started throbbing and she pressed her temples. Aside from dealing with her aunt's condition, she would have to run Juliette's business, an overwhelming notion.

He added, "The hospital and treatment are free; she will be fine. And you, Mademoiselle? Will you be all right?"

She paused, grope for words: how could she even start to explain the problems she had to face at the dress shop ... clients ... bills ... rent to pay ... she could not describe the flood of thoughts and emotions that gripped her.

He stared at her for a moment before saying, "There are some nuns who can help." He nodded toward the hallway.

This took her aback; he was referring to the Sisters of Charity. No matter how dire, her family never asked for charity. They worked; they coped; they survived. The idea that this doctor who had made them wait forever thought they were a charity case infuriated her—she had been smarting from the earlier exchange with the nurse in any case—and she snapped, "My aunt owns a dress shop on Avenue Bouquet, Doctor; I'll have you know we are not destitute." She should have stopped right there but didn't: "We waited half the day for you, Doctor, four hours, while my aunt's leg swelled to twice its normal size. She was in agony, and here we were in this God-awful place. Please make sure her leg is fine."

His face turned darkly serious. He lifted his eyebrows and chewed his lower lip for a second before speaking in the most clinical tone: Mademoiselle, be informed that there is still danger of bone necrosis although this is unlikely ...

the nurse will give you further information. And then he dismissed her: Well, then, good-day Mademoiselle, it was—he paused before continuing —a pleasure meeting you, I have to attend to others who have been waiting for longer than you have.

Melisande could have been petrified by the situation she now found herself in—alone to solve what seemed like insurmountable problems—but she knew she had to keep her wits about her. She had learned back in Lyon that when catastrophes happen, you have to deal with it. After her father died, she had helped her brother run the farm, and at night she and her mother stitched linens to make extra money. When her mother passed away, Melisande turned over the house and farm to her brother, and she packed her things into a bag and took the train to Paris. That April she did what she had to do: after making sure her aunt was all right at the Hopital Dieu de Paris, she went straight to their seamstress, Simone, and asked her to work extra hours. The next day Melisande informed their clients about Juliette's accident, and she sat down and figured out her finances, which fortunately were sound. Every afternoon she visited her aunt; and every morning and most evenings, she worked.

When life settled into a routine and was therefore less overwhelming, she felt guilty at having flung sharp words at Doctor Martine. She tried to find him at the hospital to apologize, but the few times she saw him, he was far away and very busy. On one occasion, she caught a glimpse of him, at a distance, saying goodbye to her aunt, and their eyes met, and she hurried toward them, hoping she could make things right, but before she got there, he had walked away.

That was when Juliette showed Melisande a charcoal drawing of a row of tulips. "Look Melisande, from Doctor Martine himself," she said, smiling happily and cocking her head to one side to admire the work. "He did this himself at the Jardin de Tuileries. Imagine Melisande, he is not only a surgeon but an artist." Juliette carefully propped it up on her side table.

Melisande studied the drawing and thought it was not very good; it looked like cheap artwork sold by student artists on the Left Bank. She had to control herself from making a face and criticizing it.

More drawings appeared of gardens, parks, and the bridges of the Seine, and Juliette could talk of nothing but the doctor: Doctor Martine did the morning rounds at six ... Doctor Martine took his time with each patient (with her certainly) ... Doctor Martine was thirty-five years old and unmarried ... Doctor Martine was an honors graduate from the medical school of the University of Paris ... Doctor Martine was an excellent surgeon, very clever and  absolutely delightful ... and oh, Doctor Martine was very handsome ... how very lucky she was. The broken leg seemed to have been forgotten.

Her aunt's adulation for Doctor Martine made Melisande wonder if something was going on between them. He was younger, true, but Melisande was aware that in Paris, age was not a hindrance to love. Parisians treasured the story of their King Henry's lifelong love affair with his courtesan Diane de Poitiers who was nine years older.

Two months passed and in late June, Juliette was well enough to return home with crutches. Melisande had prepared a room for her, at the back of the dress shop, away from the workers and customers. But her aunt flat-out refused to stay there. "What is wrong with my own bedroom, Melisande?" she said, referring to her room upstairs.

"You cannot climb the stairs. You cannot, not with those crutches. You must not," Melisande said.

"I can and I will," Juliette said and started climbing the stairs.

"Tante!" Melisande said as she watched her aunt ascend step by step, grimacing in pain, awkwardly struggling to keep her balance. Twice, Juliette stumbled but fortunately caught herself. All Melisande could do was trail behind her, ready to soften her fall if her aunt missed a step.

When at last Juliette was ensconced in her bedroom, Melisande insisted that she stay put. Melisande was strict —garrulous even—

in forbidding her to use the stairs. Juliette reluctantly agreed, but consequently Simone and Melisande had to go up and down countless times a day to bring the older woman what she needed. There was no choice—her aunt couldn't afford another tumble.

Between taking care of her aunt and running the dress shop, Melisande could barely keep up. One Saturday after Juliette had returned home, Melisande was still working on a bias cut skirt that required a lot of work space. She decided to use the floor instead of the cutting-table. She rolled out a bolt of moire, and after hiking up her own skirt, got down on her knees to lay down the pattern. She was cutting the fabric when she heard knocking on the door. It was late afternoon. It had been a warm day and Melisande

had left it ajar. When she looked up, there was Doctor Martine studying her. "Mademoiselle, do you need help?" he asked.

He had caught her on all fours. Embarrassed, she clambered up and brushed the lint off her skirt.

"It's me, Doctor Martine," he said, as if it were necessary to identify himself.

She had only seen him with his white coat, which made him look washed-out and undistinguishable from the other doctors. Without it he looked different—younger and his features seemed more pronounced. Her aunt was right; he was attractive after all, with strong jaws and a faint five-o'clock shadow, which looked charming, not unkempt. Because her life revolved around fabric and stitchery, she noticed the fine quality of his suit, a cashmere-wool blend it seemed, which made him look elegant.

But his unexpected appearance had unnerved her and Melisande was unable to speak.

"I've come to check your aunt's leg," he said.

"Please come in," she said. Her hair was in wild disarray with curls falling in front of her eyes, and which she tried to sweep back. Painfully, she remembered her compromising position of bending up and down and crawling on the floor—

how much of her acrobatics had the doctor noticed?

To her relief, he behaved as if nothing were wrong. Inside the shop, he studied her project on the floor. "So this is how a dress is made?" he asked.

"I should have worked at the table," she said, pointing out the clutter on the floor.

Melisande was sorry she had not tidied up —there were bolts of fabric leaning against the walls; dresses on hangers or folded and piled high on tables and chairs; sewing notions and magazines scattered about; in addition, two of their mannequins were undressed.

His eyes swept over everything.

"I'm sorry for all the clutter; I've been busy."

"Please, Mademoiselle, don't worry. I should be the one apologizing for barging in on you." He had barely finished his sentence when something caught his attention at

the table. "Drawings. May I?" he said and he leafed through sketches of dress designs, which Melisande had done. Other dress designers used stick figures in their sketches, but she drew human figures.

"I sometimes pick up my mother's clothes at the Maison Orientale, but I had no idea what went into the making of those dresses." He held up some drawings, "Did you do these?"

She nodded. "Some summer designs."

"I have noticed your artistic bent but didn't realize you also draw."

She leaned over to have a closer look at the sketches. "That is part of what we do. We design dresses for our clients and get them done."

"What is that?" he suddenly asked, sniffing and lifting his chin to locate the source. "A pleasant scent, like citrus."

She had rinsed her hair with lemon juice that morning but it seemed an intimate matter to mention that so she ignored his question. "When I arrived Paris, Tante Juliette asked me to design some spring dresses. She handed me a pile of dress design books and magazines, told me to look them over, and gave me paper and pencil. I did as I was instructed. That was all the training I got."

"Hmmm ... the figures are well-proportioned and the drawing is well-done," he said, sounding surprised. "Drawing the human figure is difficult, at least for me. I've never worked with models, but I understand one must first lay down the action line." By this time, Melisande was leading him to the stairs in the back of the shop.

He paused and tilted his head upward to size up the flight of narrow uneven steps. "Is Madame upstairs?" His voice had turned serious.

Melisande sensed the shift in his tone and demeanor.

"Her leg is not yet healed," he said with a frown.

She knew what he was thinking because those had been her thoughts exactly—it was dangerous for her aunt to be climbing stairs. His words sounded like a reprimand. Suddenly she felt tired, simply exhausted. She had been taking care of her aunt, catering to her clients, buying the groceries, supervising the seamstress, doing everything to keep things running, and here this man stood, suggesting she had maltreated her aunt. It was really too much to swallow, and her voice was shaking as she said: "She insisted. The minute she arrived, she started climbing the stairs. She defied me. I argued with her but she ignored me totally. You do not know my aunt, Doctor, she is hard-headed and impossible. She is like a child. I did my best; I am doing my best. It is not my fault that she is upstairs. It is not fair to suggest that I have neglected her."

"Mademoiselle, words flow out of your mouth easily ... recklessly in fact," he said in that clinical tone that she had heard once before at the hospital. And he went past her and ascended the stairs.

Melisande stood by the stairwell, uncertain about how to do. Certainly she was angry and wanted to be as far away from him as she could. She considered returning to her sewing project, but she was too upset to work. Her mind had latched on to his reprimand, and worse than that, his condescension. Her aunt's voice calling her reminded her that it was highly improper to leave Juliette unchaperoned with the doctor. Reluctantly Melisande went upstairs. She slipped into her aunt's bedroom, just as the doctor scolded Juliette in a gentle voice. "Madame, I understand you climbed the stairs on your own?"

"All my things are up here, Doctor. I am more comfortable in my own bedroom." Juliette fluffed her hair and arranged the neckline of her dress to lower it. She was sitting on her bed, leaning against pillows. Her outstretched legs were covered by a white crocheted blanket. Her room was rose pink in color with a lot of lace and ruffles. It was usually tidy and spacious, but now there was an extra table with her food tray, some fruit and drink. Another table had been brought up for her sewing notions. Magazines were piled high on the chair beside her bed.

"You cannot afford a fall. The bone has not mended fully." His tone was cajoling.

"Doctor Martine, I did not fall, I will not fall." Juliette nodded toward Melisande. "My niece makes sure I have everything I need. I am very lucky to have her with me. For years I had begged her to leave Lyon and join me here in Paris, but she had all sort of excuses. But now she's here. She ensures I do my exercises; she even massages my legs."

Doctor Martine turned to Melisande. He had an eyebrow up and a little smile as if he were surprised or amused or contemptuous—Melisande wasn't sure which. Words bubbled up to her throat, "Tante, Doctor Martine thinks I have been cruel to you."

Before Juliette could answer, he shot back, "That is not what I said, Madame, although indeed I was appalled at those dangerous steps, which you navigated in your delicate condition. Madame ... Mademoiselle, I had a patient who traumatized his leg a second time and there were complications. I had to deal with this unpleasant business earlier today."

Juliette closed her eyes and flung one arm over her forehead.

"Not everyone is as fortunate as you, Madame. What I mean is your leg is healing beautifully, and therefore you must take good care of yourself." In the coldest clipped voice, he added, "People should learn to control their temper."

There was a long pause as Juliette stared first at one, then the other, settling finally on Melisande, whom she pierced with her gaze. Having done that, she turned her attention back to the doctor, and in a voice lilting with charm said, "I'm up here because I chose to be here, Doctor. It was my fault. Please do not blame my niece. She is overworked, running here and there, and despite all that, succeeding in giving me excellent care. Frankly, Doctor, I don't know what I would have done without her. The truth is she is like a daughter to me."

"Like a sister, you mean. You are too young, Madame," he said, while Juliette giggled and patted her hair.

Melisande, who had felt the sting of his words, held her tongue for her aunt's sake.

"Madame, I need to check your leg." Doctor Martine cleared the chair and sat down near Juliette.

Juliette lifted the crocheted blanket to reveal not one, but both legs. He felt the bone of her leg and declared she was healing nicely. She went on to complain about some pain in her hip, and glanced up at him expectantly. The doctor did not check her hip, but said the discomfort was normal. He explained it was because of the uneven weight on both feet. Juliette went on to praise him and she kept up her coquetry, until finally Melisande had had enough. She turned to leave, but when she walked past him, he reached out and touched her arm. "Mademoiselle, stay. I need your opinion about something."

She shot him a glance, surprised at his request. But the truth was she was tired of the little game he and her aunt were playing, and she took another step toward the door. "Please stay," he said, softly. It was a plea not a command.

Juliette covered her legs with the blanket. "There is nothing important downstairs, Melisande.

You can stay, can you not?"

Melisande sat on the stool next to the window. Outside the usual din of Paris had quieted down.

"My niece is typical Lyonnais, Doctor," Juliette said, as she smiled at Doctor Martine.

Melisande glared at her aunt who was oblivious. Juliette's statement echoed the Parisian put down— Lyonnais were only good at making silk and sausages. If Melisande were not seated far from the door, she would have left, but she was trapped, and she would have to tolerate these two, for how long, she had no idea. Melisande remembered how vexed her mother used to be over Juliette. Her Maman had few good things to say about Juliette and would sometimes gossip about Juliette's many lovers and how eventually they always grew tired of her carping—where were you last Saturday ... you did not visit me ... you promised ... and so on. One of them was a wealthy man who had given her money to start her dress shop, but like the others that one eventually took off with a more agreeable woman.

"I want to show both of you something," the doctor said, his words, bringing Melisande back to the room. He had picked up his briefcase and was rifling through his papers. He sounded buoyant, optimistic, and Melisande waited to hear what he had to say. "Ah, here it is," he said, his face lighting up. He pulled out a charcoal drawing of the Eiffel Tower and held it up for Melisande to see. "What do you think?" he asked, like a child proudly showing off his school work. "Your aunt says you are very artistic and I must admit that your sketches downstairs are impressive. I would like your candid thoughts. As well as Madame's of course."

"Indeed she is very talented, Doctor," Juliette said. "If you could see her dress creations and if you understood dress design at all, you would appreciate how cleverly she works with the principles of design: emphasis, harmony, balance, rhythm. For instance, Doctor, she chooses a point of emphasis so that the best body part of a woman is enhanced. The plump one becomes voluptuous; the rail-thin one sophisticated. Melisande works with texture, color and shape to give a feeling of oneness. My niece has extraordinary abilities."

Her aunt's praise took the sting out of her earlier Lyonnais-statement, and Melisande was grateful for her aunt's words. She was also glad that the doctor heard that she was not a mere seamstress. She was sick and tired of Parisian condescension.

"And that is why I would like your opinion of my work, both of you," Doctor Martine said.

Juliette spoke before Melisande did. "Pooh!" she said, with her nose scrunched. "I am not a fan of the Eiffel. It is too modern, Doctor Martine!"

The doctor looked amused.

Encouraged, her aunt continued, "I remember watching them build it platform by platform, from '87 to '89. I prayed it would get better—or topple down—but the higher it went, the more hideous it became. The skyline of Paris has been ruined by that ghastly protrusion."

"It's Gustave Eiffel's most famous work," he said.

"He should have stuck to making bridges. Oh, how I abhor his tower. I'm not talking about the drawing because you're an excellent artist and I love your work. I'm referring to the subject you chose, a monstrosity."

He remained mirthful when he said, "Blame Koehlin and Nouguier, Madame. They made the original design for Eiffel's company."

Juliette continued her lament. "The tower is useless. It's an aberration that does not fit the other structures in Paris. You heard of course that the writer Guy de Maupassant used to have his lunch in the tower's restaurant daily to avoid seeing the structure?"

Melisande passed by the Eiffel Tower several times a day. It had a presence that could not be ignored. She had felt it the first time she saw it, looking gray and slick in the rain. When she was new in Paris, on many occasions she used the Eiffel as her beacon to guide her back to the shop. It was reliable, fixed. This was the first time she heard of its controversies and was interested.

"I can see the Eiffel from my window," he said. "I'm afraid, Madame, it has worked its charm on me. I find it most appealing. It has a certain beauty. Consider that it's made of metal and yet it manages to be delicate and graceful. And throughout the day, as the sun moves, its appearance changes. The shadows it casts alter the landscape as well. It is like a woman that way—changeable and seductive."

"The 'Iron Lady' they call it, Doctor, but tell me, what is feminine about a rigid structure thrusting up in the middle of Paris like a gigantic phallus?—"

Melisande covered her mouth in shock—her aunt could really be outrageous! No wonder she and her Maman did not get along.

"—Nothing soft, no folds, all angles and symmetry."

And there he was, laughing and watching her. "And you, Mademoiselle—what do you think? Not about the Eiffel, but about my work because that was why I kept you here. Feel free to speak your mind. I am certain that a brilliant woman like you will have a lot to say. I can take your criticism, Mademoiselle." He squared his jaw as if bracing himself.

Melisande oftentimes felt like a country bumpkin in Paris, and she didn't miss that he had explicitly asked for her opinion. She had also noted his praise for her. If she looked at the matter clearly; if she set aside the annoying flirtation between him and her aunt, well, he had done nothing wrong really. She was the one with the short fuse. He had taken excellent care of her aunt; and here he was, making sure her leg was healing, and amusing her with his art and chitchat.

"Mademoiselle?"

Melisande weighed her words so as not to offend him. "When I arrived, the Eiffel was already here, so to me it is part of Paris. It does not offend me, but neither do I love it as you do, Doctor. But about your artwork, I can see that it is—how do I put it?—well done." The truth was that she found his drawing simplistic and lacking in imagination. "Very well rendered," she added, to conclude the matter.

"And—?"

"It is a faithful copy of the Eiffel." She had nothing else good to say about it.

"Mademoiselle, please stop censoring yourself. Go ahead; tell me. You can see that I'm a grown man."

Her aunt knew Melisande could be blunt and she rolled her eyes and said, "Ooh la la!"

Melisande took a deep breath. "Forgive me, Doctor, I will try my best, but I don't always have the words to express myself. While your work is rendered very well, it seems to be ... hmm ... lacking something." She paused, wondering how to tell him that his work was lifeless.

"Please continue, Mademoiselle," the doctor said.

"When I look at something created by someone—a creation that is—I want to feel something. An emotion must bubble up inside me. You understand me?"

He nodded, listening to every word she said.

"My heart must be touched; my soul must quiver; memories must be unlocked or formed. Nothing of this sort happens when I look at this drawing. It looks like the other drawings sold near the Eiffel. Executed very well, you understand, but so are those other drawings."

As she talked the expectant expression on his face slowly faded, and by the time she finished, he looked pale. She wondered if she had overstepped herself. Had she been reckless with her words, as he had accused her? She needed to learn to talk the way Juliette did, in a teasing voice, even as she ripped someone apart. Melisande felt flustered ... and ... she felt sorry for him.

His voice was flat when he replied, "Interesting idea, about feeling. I never studied art. I was too busy with the sciences. I started drawing because I discovered it allowed me to rest."

With a weary expression, he opened his briefcase to return his work. (Melisande noted he did not give this to her aunt, not after hearing her vehemence about the Eiffel).

He continued, "You can imagine that some patients do not survive or that they end up badly. My patient this morning who lost his leg—I had difficulty dealing with that. His wife and children will also suffer. It's not just one life, but many lives affected by such tragedies."

Juliette, who liked to believe that everything should be sunny and nice, never dark and sad, said in a cheerful voice, "It's good that you have turned to art to keep from dwelling on such dreary matters, Doctor. You are one step ahead of Leonardo da Vinci. He studied anatomy to improve his art; you already know anatomy. But you must keep in mind that the judgment of your work came from two dress designers. Granted Melisande is an artist in her haute couture, but she is not an art expert. With a little bit of this and a little bit of that, she and I can create the illusion that a woman is beautiful."

That day, Melisande was wearing a raw silk dress, turquoise in color with magenta piping at the hem, understated but cool, perfect for a summer day, and he looked at it and said, "Yes, you have a good eye. The colors are interesting, and you play with texture too." He paused— "Now, feeling? Do I feel something when I look at your creation? Yes, I feel happy knowing we will have beautiful days ahead. In a flash, I recalled past summers, but it was not a full recollection, it was more like the scent of perfume, flitting, something that cannot be contained. And a memory has now been formed of my being here with the two of you this summer afternoon."

"Voila! You are learning," Juliette said.

He seemed to have recovered and his voice had a lift once more. "I like the idea that art should create feelings. It is profound, in fact. I have been preoccupied with acquiring the skills but did not consider creating feeling in my work; or should I say creating work with feeling?"

Her aunt continued her banter. "You are interested in the subtle changes of the Iron Lady. Clearly there is something in your mind and in your heart about the Eiffel. Let us see if we can get to it. Let's play a little game, Doctor. Close your eyes and tell me what you see."

Sometimes Juliette and Melisande did this before sketching a dress; it allowed their minds free reign to come up with fresh ideas. But imagination seemed contrary to the nightmare of broken bodies and pain and medicines. Melisande wondered how he would respond. She expected him to balk, but he closed his eyes.

The days were now longer, and through the window, the sun's rays slanted in and shone on his dark hair. His face was as still as that of a statue, and his eyelashes were crescent fringes on his cheeks. She felt like touching them with one finger as one touches a caterpillar—gently. He had talked about his Eiffel Tower changing but it was he who was always changing, from a doctor to an artist, from a jovial man, to a serious one, to one who brooded over broken people—what else would they learn about him? There was something hidden in that face, something exotic and different, something fascinating.

"Well then, Doctor Martine?"

It was as if he had left them for a long time, and it wasn't until the church bells tolled that his eyes fluttered open.

"Doctor?"

He took a deep breath and sat forward. "That was interesting. It's the first time I've experienced anything like that. It was very restful. I even feel I've recovered from the harsh criticism of my work."

Juliette moaned. "Oh, Doctor Martine, please do not take our words to heart!"

He smiled and waved his hand to indicate he was jesting. "I did not actually see anything. It was more of a feeling." He started gathering his things.

"You can't leave now, not until you tell us what you saw," Juliette said.

He paused, "I felt there was a woman in front of the Eiffel tower."

"A woman? How mysterious! Then you must do the drawing so you can find out more about this."

"I have done only one portrait, in oil, poorly done, I'm afraid. I have books that teach me what to do, but I need to practice drawing live models. As you can guess, Madame, I am up early in the morning, I do rounds, surgery, and there is paperwork to complete. I also have my parents to attend to. Art lessons require time. I've looked into it, and it's impossible."

Juliette pursed her lips as if weighing matters. She finally said, "You know, Doctor Martine, we are here. When we are free, you can practice drawing us, my niece and myself. I do not mind. But as you can see, I am stuck up here." She swept her hands over her legs and gave a wry expression. "However, my niece's legs are not broken; she can stand in front of the Eiffel if that is the image in your head. She is young, she can pose for hours until your work is perfect."

Melisande, surprised at what her aunt had said, folded her hands and remained still.

He threw her a questioning look. She said nothing but neither did she protest.

He went to Juliette to kiss her hand and say goodbye. "I would like my art to improve. My art feeds a part of myself that is vital, and which is unfortunately starved at the hospital. Mademoiselle and I had some bad starts but hopefully she has forgiven me?"

Melisande did not reply but inside she felt they were on good ground.

Juliette arranged herself against the pillows before she said, "Melisande, before the doctor leaves, can you get one of our silk scarves? They're downstairs in a box behind the counter. The Doctor's mother may like one." She was referring to the scarves that they gave away as gifts to special clients.

As Melisande was making her way downstairs, she overheard Juliette say, "I like you, Doctor Martine. You have been very kind to me. I will tell you something in confidence: Melisande could have been my daughter indeed. Her father was very handsome—ooh la la!—I was madly in love with him—" and here she laughed before continuing in her lilting pleasant voice, "But it did not end up well, at least not for me. As the saying goes, my heart was broken. And oh, Doctor, believe me hearts take longer to heal than bones. I will give her permission to sit for you, but remember that she is someone precious to me and I do not want her hurt."

"The god Zeus must have been afraid of you and him," the doctor said. "You know the story told by Plato, do you not?" He continued talking but Melisande was now in the supply room and could no longer make out his words.

The young woman selected a lovely pink scarf and wrapped it in a box. Now she understood why her Maman disliked her aunt and why Juliette had left Lyon for Paris. Melisande wondered if her father had loved her too. About Juliette's offer to the doctor for her to sit as his model, she wasn't sure what to make of it. It didn't seem a big matter to sit for him—he had been most helpful to her aunt after all, and he could be amiable. She supposed he would want to talk about art; on that matter, they were equals.

Melisande returned to the room and handed the box to her aunt who in turn gave it to the doctor. "For your mother, Doctor," Juliette said. He took the gift and thanked her, then he turned to Melisande. "Perhaps one Sunday, if you are free, you can sit for me? But I will try to learn all I can beforehand, so I don't waste your time—" He stopped and shook his head, "No, I'm not being honest—it's so your comments may be less scathing. But I value what you have to say and you must feel free to tell me the truth." He took Melisande's hand and kissed it, his breath passing over it like a summer breeze.

Melisande caught her aunt hide her smile.

Before the doctor left, he told Juliette she could now put fifty percent weight on the leg, but that she had to continue using crutches, and she had to avoid using the stairs.

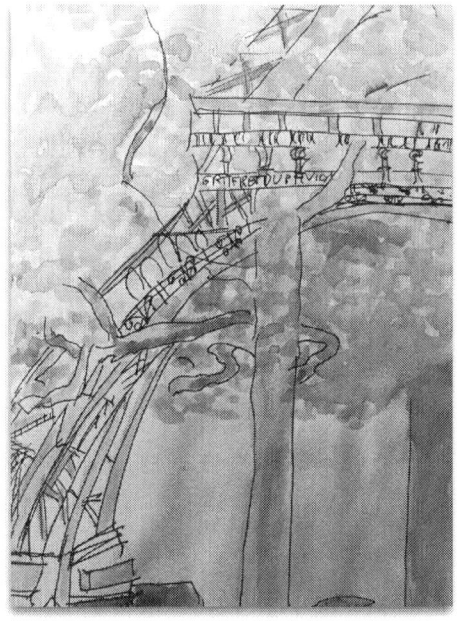

And so one Sunday, after stopping by the patisserie to pick up some cakes, Melisande arrived at his flat. After his visit where he had caught her working on the floor, he had continued to stop by to "check her aunt's leg." He was always solicitous of Juliette but he also took time to discuss his progress in art with Melisande. He confessed that he had been reading art books and doing simple sketches of people to improve his drawing. He waited several weeks before he asked Melisande to sit, and there she was navigating four flights of stairs, narrow, winding and dark. Remembering how quickly her aunt had lost her balance when she broke her leg, she hung on to the bannisters and carefully negotiated the stairs. Each floor had two apartments, but she saw no one and she wondered where people had gone to this Sunday morning.

Up and up she climbed and when she reached the top, suddenly there was light that burst through the darkness. Looking up she saw a huge skylight that glowed like the moon. The golden brilliance gave her a feeling of lightness, of joy, and she savored the moment. Melisande was still spellbound when suddenly the door opened and there he stood, Doctor Samir Martine, holding a metal whisk. Using the whisk, he pointed upward. "I had that put in," he said. "I had a difficult time finding the right person who could do it, but here it is. What do you think?"

"It's very nice," Melisande said, politely.

"Nice? Nice? It is fantastic. Come in. Watch how, aside from being one of the best surgeons in Paris, I am also one of the best cooks."

His kitchen and dining area occupied a huge space that opened out to a small balcony. It was painted yellow so that the brightness you experienced in the hallway, carried through in this room and on to the balcony outside. Melisande could see the Eiffel Tower in the distance, its gray latticed metal gleaming in the early morning sun. The trees and bushes of Paris were still in bloom. The paulownia trees surrounding the Eiffel were heavy with purple flowers. He pointed these out to her, and he showed Melisande where he wanted her to sit so he could catch the tower and the trees in the background. The chair and easel were in place. "But first, breakfast," he announced.

He bustled about in the kitchen, while she stood, uncomfortably clutching her wrap against her chest. She remembered how poor she and her mother had been in Lyon, and how they never had the luxury of having Sunday breakfast together. Sunday was the day they went to the market to sell the linens she and her mother had done. It came to her then that her mother would have liked this doctor, just as her aunt did.

She hadn't realize how stiff and awkward she must have appeared until he left the kitchen, walked to her, removed her wrap, and said, "Come, let us put this down." He lay it on a side table with a pile of art books, then he handed her a knife and basket and pointed at the baguette. "You are in charge of the bread and cheese. I'm in charge of the important part of breakfast."

His manner was easy and the way he talked made her want to laugh. His ease as he cooked impressed her. How meticulous he was as he picked up each egg from the basket, held this up to the light before cracking it into a bowl. He beat the eggs and proceeded to cook his omelet, soft and fluffy and warm, and before they sat down to eat, he placed a pat of butter on top.

He also had warm bread, cheese, some raspberries, and delicious strong coffee, which came from a Brazilian patient of his. "Broken wrist," he said, "but I also fixed it perfectly."

Afterwards, he opened a bottle of champagne, from another patient. "And what was wrong with this one?" she dared ask, as she sipped from the glass he offered her.

"Nothing broken. He started to have difficulties walking. I taught him some exercises, and I told him to stop eating aubergine which is bad for arthritis."

The champagne was getting to her head and she was surprised when she teased him. "You know everything, then."

"No, not everything. About doctoring, yes, but not about art. I thought a lot about what you said about feeling in art. I've spent a lot of time preparing for today. My technique has improved. So today we will see if I can draw you, the Eiffel, and have feeling in the work, all at the same time."

He looked out at the sky and said the light was perfect. He led her out to the balcony, sat her down, and directed her to turn here and there to catch the light as he wanted it. He had requested that Melisande wear her white peasant blouse—he had seen it during a visit—cotton, gathered with strings that tie in front, long sleeves, quite simple. She had no idea why he preferred this instead of something prettier. In any case there she sat while he cocked his head to the right and to the left. Suddenly, he placed his charcoal down. "I saw an oil painting of a woman with this type of blouse—it was a Dutch painting—but she was not so—how do I put it?—stiff. She looked relaxed. It looked less studied, random in a way, and very interesting. Do not misunderstand, but would it be all right, if you loosen the strings so the fabric flows better?"

And since she did not do so to his satisfaction, he came near her, "May I?" And he adjusted the blouse, his fingers touching her—warm, fleeting, like the sudden brush of a feather. She must have reacted because he said, "Pardon," but he made nothing of it and resumed his post in front of the easel. His right hand clutched the charcoal and moved furiously while his eyes moved from Melisande to the paper then back to her.

The sun's rays felt good and she felt herself surrendering to the morning on that balcony. She felt mesmerized. She lifted her chin higher to meet the sunlight and her body relaxed.

He nodded when she did that but said nothing. He appeared lost in his work. Melisande knew the feeling of being totally absorbed in one's work; she could get that way too when she was engrossed in her projects, and she would feel as if she were far away in another planet. Trying not to disturb him, she glanced away and saw that he had a birdfeeder attached to the railing at the other end of the balcony. It amused her to think that he had time to feed wild birds. Two red breasted robins were pecking away at the seeds. She looked out beyond them, at Paris that was waking up, the streets not as busy this Sunday morning. She remembered the conversation he had with her aunt about the Eiffel Tower. She had to agree with him that the tower was charming—yes, made of hard metal but it had grace as it peaked up to the blue summer sky of Paris, like a finger pointing to eternity.

"No," he interrupted her, "don't look out there, turn towards me, please. There must be communication between the subject and artist, otherwise, I might as well be drawing a vase."

Melisande did as she was told and she observed his face, the furrowed brow, his intense dark eyes. She had gotten used to seeing him smiling and tossing out his boastful funny comments; this studious expression was new. He looked as if he were in prayer. The way the sunlight struck his hair made it seem lighter and created the illusion of a halo around his head. Now and then he would say, "Don't move," or "Lift the chin higher." Otherwise, they said little to each other, and after a while, Melisande felt like an inanimate object and she wondered if he would end up with work that was a faithful rendering but lifeless. To amuse herself she imagined dress designs and accessories for the fall, but he called her attention back. "Please, look at me."

She did, and the longer she stared at him, the more she liked his serious face. There was something going on inside him, something deeper than his flippant remarks, or his doctoring, or his art, something else.

Just when she felt she could no longer hold her position, he said, "Come, take a look."

Her muscles had tightened and when she stood up, she twisted her body and extended her arms. He too moved his neck and shook his arms, and the familiarity of stretching together made them smile.

"Come." His voice had turned low with undertones. He beckoned her and she went to him. The balcony was narrow and they stood very close to each other.

Melisande knew that she was not a bad-looking woman, but she had never considered herself beautiful. There were many women more attractive, especially in Paris, but the woman in his drawing surprised her. This was the image: Melisande was twenty-two years old, wearing a long flowing skirt and the off-shoulder cotton blouse. Her long hair flowed around her, her face caught the sun's rays, and she had an expression that was lazy and happy, and her mouth was slightly open, and her eyes had the expression of longing.

Earlier that morning, while getting dressed, she had thought the billowy blouse had been modest, frumpy in fact, but his picture showed all the curves of her breasts. She stepped away in embarrassment and crossed her arms in front of chest.

"You are not happy with it? I've been working hard to get better." He was frowning, clearly unhappy.

She could not find the right words to tell him that the picture showed a sensuous woman, far more sensuous than she considered herself to be, so she turned away from him, but he touched her arm, and asked, "What is wrong? Please tell me."

"The drawing is well done—"

"You said that about my drawing of the Eiffel," he said, "Does this one also lack feeling?"

"No, not that. It makes me feel many things. Pride, shame ... no, not exactly shame, but something like it."

"Shame!" His voice rose. "Ashamed because you are beautiful. Such foolishness." He was clearly cross and he turned away to wipe his hands on a rag, but he suddenly stopped. "Melisande, come here," he said. He drew her close, and with his large hands he touched her face, every part of it, slowly as if he were a blind man committing to memory her face—his fingers molding her cheeks, her forehead, her eyebrows, her lips, his fingers sliding down to her neck, to her shoulders. He slid her blouse to one side, exposing more of her shoulder, and he bent down to kiss it, his warm breath lingering on her skin even after he straightened his back.

It was there in front of them, Desire, and her breath caught as she wondered what he would do next. In Lyon, when Melisande was eighteen, Etienne and she had made love in the barn—clumsy and hasty lest they be caught. That had been her first experience with a man. She didn't know much about making love, but she was certain that there was something that hovered in that balcony, this Desire for the other, and the feeling was so intense she thought surely something further would happen. But to her surprise, he resumed gathering his things and brought them inside.

Not knowing what to do with herself, she proceeded to tie her blouse together but he returned and stopped her. "Leave it that way. Come in," he said. "It's almost noon. Shadows are harsh at this time now. Can you carry the easel?" His hands were full of the other art supplies.

She picked up the easel and followed him to a room where he organized his art materials in a long bookcase against one wall. The other walls were covered with his artwork and when he saw that she was interested, he pointed out recent portraits of the butcher and the fruit vendor.

He was leaving the room when she caught sight of a solitary portrait near an alcove and she strayed briefly to have a closer look. It was an oil painting of an Arabic woman. The painting was crudely done, but Melisande could see that the woman was attractive and exotic, in her flowing skirt and heavily beaded top. A thin veil covered her mouth and chin, as if she came straight from the deserts of Arabia. Her back faced the painter, but her head was turned to the side so you could see three-quarters of her veiled face. The gossamer-thin veil revealed her face, mysterious and sensuous. And her figure cut a most charming shape, as if she were caught mid-stream in a belly-dance. The sight of this incredible woman filled Melisande with pain and jealousy. Doctor Martine had been visiting her and her aunt regularly, which made her feel to some extent that they owned him. Now she realized he had ties with other people, with this woman for instance, for surely his careful

rendering of this beautiful woman indicated that they had a relationship. Melisande was certain he loved her.

The brightness of the morning left her, and in its place was a painful somberness. She caught up with him and she primly declared that it was time for her to go home. Moving like a puppet, she searched for her wrap and bag. She was poised to leave when he touched her arm and in a soft voice said, "Please don't leave."

"It is almost noon. My aunt will be waiting for me." In her distress her voice quivered, and she had to struggle to hold back her tears. At that moment, she felt foolish thinking that an important surgeon like him could care for a dressmaker like her.

He looked perplexed. "Something happened, and I have no idea what it is. Your aunt will be fine. I have some nice arugula and goat cheese, and sausage. We still have bread and the cakes you brought. Let us have lunch, and explain to me why you are now upset. I need to understand what happened. You know, do you not, that I would never hurt you?" Gently, he removed her wrap and folded it, and he took away her bag as well.

Melisande did not protest. He mesmerized her. His presence was big and overpowering. She thought she had loved Etienne, but this was a feeling that was greater than that. It frightened her; this power that he had over her.

After banishing her things to his bedroom, he was back, and sounding like a captain, he told her to sit at the dining table and watch him make the best salad in Paris. Like a magician, he proceeded to throw together another wonderful meal, and he opened a bottle of red wine, and he chit-chatted about the people whose portraits he had done and the good weather they had been having, and later he cajoled her, trying to get her to explain why her mood had changed.

"It is nothing," Melisande began, determined not to tell him the truth, but remembering the mysterious veiled woman made tears spring to her eyes.

His dining table was round, not very large, and he placed his fork down and reached across the table. He swept away some tendrils of hair from her face, and he wiped away her tears. This tenderness made her weep even more and she sat there quietly sobbing.

"We had a nice breakfast, you posed for me, and it's true I made you sit too long. Could you be unhappy about that?"

She shook my head.

He continued, "Perhaps you were offended that I ... I ... took some liberties?"

He was referring to his kissing her shoulder, and she said nothing. The truth was that she enjoyed his admiration and desire for her. It was the woman in the painting who had upset her, who made her feel he belonged to some other woman, that she could never have him. She wondered if he was simply playing with emotions, and what kind of cruel man could do such a thing.

Then perhaps he reviewed what had transpired that morning, and it came to him: "You saw her picture? The woman with the veil?" He smiled and said, "She is my mother. I found a daguerreotype of her and made a painting from it. She was from Oran, in Algiers. Her name is Yasmin. My father was a surgeon, like myself; or I should say I became a surgeon like my father. He was assigned there. They met and fell in love. My mother's family were descendants of Muhammad; they, in particular, were not happy about my father. It is a long story and one day I will tell you all about how they overcame all obstacles. But for now, I have some nice bonbons from a beautiful nurse ..."

Melisande frowned.

"... who is older than my mother, and she gave me these because she says she enjoys working with me most of all because I am the best surgeon in Paris."

His audacity made her laugh. "Do you always have such a high opinion of yourself," she asked.

"Of course. One must believe in one's self. You have to believe in yourself. In your beauty, in your strength, and courage, your intelligence. I see all these in you."

His words made her face flush, and she turned away. He had a way of making her feel self-conscious. "Don't stare at me so," she said.

"Why not? I enjoy looking at you," he said.

"It makes me feel ... how do I put it ... embarrassed?"

"No, you should not feel that way. I don't want to embarrass you. I want to talk to you and make you laugh. I want to make you happy," he said. They had finished eating, and he had gotten up to start clearing the table. She helped him, and together they washed the dishes and put them away, like an old couple, which made her smile. In the distance a clock chimed two o'clock, and quickly he said, "You're fine, you do not have to go home yet." He took away the dishtowel from her hands, and in a voice throaty with desire said, "Spend the afternoon with me. I want to give you pleasure."

He must have read that there was no protest there, no resistance because he bent down and kissed her forehead, her eyes, and then her lips. And with his hand around her waist, he led her to his bedroom with the brass bed, and he cleared away her things from the bed, and lifted her unto it.

That day, after they had made love, he told her that Plato said humans were originally created with four arms, four legs, and a head with two faces. But fearing their power, Zeus split them into two separate parts, condemning them to spend their lives in search of their other halves. Samir said that he and Melisande were very fortunate to have found each other, because they were meant to be one. He said, when they part, it will hurt them very much, because the one-ness will be separated once again.

Melisande remembered the summer afternoon when Samir had first visited her aunt—(it was the same afternoon when Melisande had fallen in love with him). Her aunt had revealed to him her thwarted love affair with Melisande's father. How broken Juliette's heart had been; hearts take longer to heal than bones, Juliette had said. Melisande understood then that what she had taken as sibling rivalry between her mother and Juliette ran deeper than that. Now, after Samir's story of the four-armed, four-legged being with two faces, Melisande saw that Juliette had not only lost a man she loved, but her other half—a vital part of herself. All these years, since Juliette left Lyon, she had existed as half-a-person. The good looks, the charm, the giggling, the coquetry were part of the sham to hide the lonely incomplete human being.

Even as she rested in Samir's arms, Melisande shivered thinking of her aunt's sad fate and she welcomed her feeling of wholeness with Samir.

Cecilia Manguerra Brainard

Cecilia first met her character Melisande in her novel, *The Newspaper Widow*.

Cecilia is the award-winning author and editor of twenty books, including the novels: *When the Rainbow Goddess Wept*, *Magdalena*; and short story collections: *Vigan and Other Stories*, *Acapulco at Sunset and Other Stories*, *Woman With Horns and Other Stories*.

Cecilia co-edited six other books and co-authored a novel, *Angelica's Daughters, a Dugtungan Novel*.

Her work has been translated into Finnish and Turkish; and many of her stories and articles have been widely anthologized.

Cecilia has received a California Arts Council Fellowship in Fiction, a Brody Arts Fund Award, a Special Recognition Award for her work dealing with Asian American youths, as well as a Certificate of Recognition from the California State Senate, 21st District. She received the prestigious Filipinas Magazine Arts Award, and the Outstanding Individual Award from her birth city, Cebu, Philippines. She has received several travel grants in the Philippines, from the USIS (United States Information Service).

She has lectured and performed in worldwide literary arts organizations and universities, including UCLA, USC, University of Connecticut, University of the Philippines, PEN, Beyond Baroque, Shakespeare & Company in Paris, and many others.

Aside from writing and editing, Cecilia publishes fine literature under the imprint of Philippine American Literary House (Palhbooks.com).

Discover more fine titles from **Philippine American Literary House (PALH)**

Growing Up Filipino: Stories for Young Adults, Edited by Cecilia Manguerra Brainard
Growing Up Filipino II: More Stories for Young Adults, Edited by Cecilia Manguerra Brainard
A River, One-Woman Deep: Stories by Linda Ty-Casper
Benedicta Takes Wing and Other Stories by Veronica Montes

PALH Kindle eBooks on Amazon
Acapulco at Sunset and Other Stories by Cecilia Manguerra Brainard
A River, One-Woman Deep: Stories by Linda Ty-Casper
A Small Party in a Garden, novel by Linda Ty-Casper
Awaiting Trespass, novel by Linda Ty-Casper

Fiction by Filipinos in America, Edited by Cecilia Manguerra Brainard
Magdalena, novel by Cecilia Manguerra Brainard
The Newspaper Widow by Cecilia Manguerra Brainard
Vigan and Other Stories by Cecilia Manguerra Brainard
When the Rainbow Goddess Wept, novel by Cecilia Manguerra Brainard
Wings of Stone, novel by Linda Ty-Casper
Woman with Horns and Other Stories by Cecilia Manguerra Brainard

PALH (Philippine American Literary House)
P.O. Box 5099
S.M., CA 90409, USA
Email: palh@aol.com; palhbooks@gmail.com

Made in the USA
Las Vegas, NV
18 September 2023